War Beneath the Sea

War
Beneath the
Sea

by Frank Bonham

THOMAS Y. CROWELL COMPANY · NEW YORK

Manufactured in the United States of America
by the Vail-Ballou Press, Inc., Binghamton, New York

LIBRARY OF CONGRESS CATALOG CARD NO. 62-12811

First Printing

An explanation of naval terms and phrases is on page 255
and a note from the author is on page 261.

The official count of United States submarines lost in World War II stands at fifty-two. Some of these were boats on their first patrol. Others were battered old World War I "Sugar-boats." All of them died carrying the battle to the enemy.

To the courageous officers and men of these ships, this book is dedicated.

1

Keith did not sleep well this first night at sea. His bunk, in a compartment which housed a dozen crewmen, was like the cots he had seen in prison movies —an iron frame hinged to a steel wall and supported by chains. The thin mattress seemed to be full of breakfast food, which crackled every time he turned over. From above and below rose clanking sounds, as though something were being manufactured aboard the freighter. Every time he dropped off to sleep, a hammer would begin to bang belowdecks, and he would waken with a groan.

The *Bataan Trader* had left Honolulu that morning with a cargo of pineapples and sugar for San Francisco. Keith Stocker was her only passenger. At first the pineapples had smelled wonderful, but already the sugary fumes from the cargo wells were beginning to nauseate him. He had tried to get passage on a regular passenger steamer, but no space had been available for months. Ever since the Japanese attack on Pearl Harbor two months ago, everyone in Hawaii seemed to be trying to get to the mainland.

The *Bataan Trader* heeled heavily on a slow swing from her course. He clutched at the bunk above him to keep from falling out of bed. Every few minutes the ship would swing from right to left or from left to right—"zigging," they called it. The maneuver was calculated to keep enemy submarines from getting a straight shot at her—not that a Japanese submarine would come ten thousand miles to sink a pineapple boat.

Some seamen came in, pulled off their shoes, and muttered as they settled into their blankets. Other seamen grumbled, pulled on their shoes, and went out, pushing aside the blackout curtain as they stepped over the high sill. For a time all was quiet. In the damp heat of the airless room, a man began to snore. Dull with fatigue, Keith gazed at the dim blue lamp above the door, wondering whether it was near dawn. The blue light of the blackout lamp reminded him of the coolness of an undersea cave. A tingle of pleasure suddenly rose through him. He closed his eyes and pretended that it was Sunday, and he had gone down to the beach with some boys from his dormitory to goggle-fish. He had swum down to a reef and was peering into a cave where a big sea bass stared out at him, while swarms of little tropical fish shimmered like butterflies. He had taken up the sport only last summer. He loved lying on the bottom while small fish nibbled his skin and big red garibaldi came fearlessly to exhibit him to their iridescent red-and-blue babies.

He tried to prolong the undersea illusion. But now another memory came. He saw black oil from sunken warships washing up on the beaches after the Japanese attack. He saw serpentines of barbed wire stretching along the beaches, and signs warning of land mines. That was what the war had done to the Islands—turned them into a battlefield and scared everybody to death. He guessed everybody in the world was scared, as World War II spread over it like a brush fire.

In the weary dusk of the compartment, Keith squinted at his wrist watch, and sighed. It was 4:30. The worst time of all—too late to sleep, too early to get up. But after a few minutes he sat up, scrubbed his face with his hands, and looked about for his clothes. He felt a need for fresh air unsweetened with pineapple. Dropping lightly to the deck, he dressed in silence. He was seventeen, compactly made, and a little under medium height, with a swimmer's cleanness of build. His face was square. He had blue eyes and a wide mouth, and sun-browned skin that made his teeth look whiter.

He tucked in his shirttail and went to the door. As he folded the blackout curtain aside a man on one of the bunks said gruffly, "Don't light no matches while you're on deck, bud. We're blacked out, you know."

Keith looked around. He could not tell who had spoken. "Okay," he said.

On deck, everything glistened with moisture. The wind carried the pineapple smell away. Overhead the sky was still black, with a thousand white clusters of stars. He walked along the railing toward the forecastle deck, reeling slightly to the roll of the ship. High up on the bow, he could see the black silhouette of an antiaircraft gun with its small crew of Navy gunners—the only warlike muscles the *Bataan Trader* could flex. The bow lifted into the stars and settled back, lifted again and rolled off to the right, ponderously.

When he leaned on the rail, the dew immediately soaked through his shirt sleeves. Hearing a door open and close, he glanced around. A man wearing an officer's cap was coming along the deck. Keith recognized the ship's mate, a big, black-haired man named Mackenzie. The mate joined him at the rail.

"Can't sleep, eh?"

"I guess I must have slept a little."

"Pretty hard to settle down, with this infernal zigging goin' on. Don't blame the old *Trader* for it. She was against this war right from the start." He put a pipe in his mouth and rattled the stem against his teeth. For a moment Keith was afraid he was

4

going to strike a match for it. But the mate merely chewed on the pipestem and gazed out to sea.

"College kid, aincha?"

"Yes. I was going to the University."

"Where you going now?"

"To Los Angeles. I'll be living with my aunt and uncle."

"Going back to school, I expect?"

"Until I'm drafted, I guess. I've only got about six months to go till I'm eighteen."

"They don't draft you till you're twenty-one."

"They'll be drafting everybody, if it lasts much longer. I may enlist instead of waiting."

"It'll last," said the mate grimly. "It's going to be a big one, this stinking war. At first I thought we'd squash these Japs like bugs. But look at 'em go! They're all over Asia and the Pacific. Even the Philippines. We'll lose Corregidor Island before long. And all the men on it."

Keith gazed out across the long, glistening furrows of the sea. A hard-cornered lump formed in his throat as he thought about Corregidor Island, in the Philippines, guardian of Manila Bay. The mate couldn't know how Keith felt about Corregidor. He had no way of knowing that Corregidor was the reason he was going home, that his father had been killed in action there last month.

"No. I guess it hasn't got a chance."

"I've seen it, son. It's solid rock, a regular ant's nest of tunnels and gun emplacements. But with the Japs surrounding it on the hills, blasting it with bombs and shore guns, what chance do our people have?"

Keith shook his head. "None," he agreed. And then he said: "My father was killed there last month, Mister Mackenzie."

Mackenzie gazed at him. Then, laying his hand on Keith's arm, he said, "I'm sorry, skipper. I put my foot in it that time, didn't I? Was he an Army man?"

"He was an infantry officer," Keith said.

Something about the darkness and the big, friendly man at his side made him want to talk. He was surprised at the way he opened up—as people talked frankly around a campfire, letting out things they might have been embarrassed to say ordinarily. He told about his mother's dying when he was nine. He mentioned the boarding schools he had lived in. He had not lived at home for years, since his father was always moving to a new post. And besides, an Army officer had no time to take care of a boy.

Then, suddenly, word had come of Colonel Stocker's death on Corregidor.

"I don't know how it happened yet," he said. "Maybe I'll get a letter from a chaplain or his commanding officer some day."

A bell rang twice, and Mister Mackenzie slapped the rail.

"Woops! Got to jump. Say, why don't you plan to have dinner with the captain and me tonight? Nothing fancy—just pull on an old sweat shirt. Do you like baked ham?"

"Yes, sir!"

"Fine. We're having it with pineapple rings." The enthusiasm faded from Keith's face, and the mate laughed. "We've got a lot of pineapple to eat between here and the mainland, skipper. Got to keep ahead of the spoilage. Be glad this ain't a banana boat—we'd be eating bananas three times a day!"

2

After the mate left, Keith stood at the rail peering through the darkness in what he thought was the direction of the Islands. For a moment he imagined he could see a glow in the sky from the lights of Honolulu; then he remembered that the lights had gone out for the duration of the war. He leaned overside to watch the bow wave sloshing aside, the clean breeze pressing against his shirt. Gazing down, he could see a big wave peeling away from the rusty side of the ship, its crest edged with blue-green foam. At times he had seen whole ranks of breakers crashing on the beach and bursting into luminescent foam like that, just the color of the radium numerals on a watch. Some sort of organism in the water, they said. When you walked on the wet sand, your footprints glowed brightly for several moments.

He gazed farther out and saw a path of phosphorescence in the water, as though a school of porpoise might be traveling on the surface. Just then he heard footfalls and glanced around to see one of the Navy gunners descending to the main deck. Carrying coffee mugs, the sailor walked toward Keith.

Keith said, "Hi." The sailor growled, "Yo!" and walked by. When Keith returned his gaze to the water, he saw that the path of luminescence was still there, but much closer and more distinct. It looked as wide as a city street. He was startled.

"Hey, sailor!" he called. "Is that a school of porpoise out there?"

The sailor took a casual glance. "No, the water always looks—"

Then he saw it. The coffee mugs crashed to the deck, and he screamed:

"Torpedo!"

He ran toward the antiaircraft gun, where two men had jumped into silhouette and were shouting, "Where? Whereaway?"

"Port quarter! Hundred yards!"

The sailor faced the bridge, abaft the cargo well. *"Torpedo!"* he bawled at the helmsman.

Paralyzed, Keith stood there dumbly.

The antiaircraft gun exploded into a flashing, deafening, shocking clamor. The blinding flashes made his eyes ache. Rings of light burst around the torpedo's blue-green wake as the gunners attempted to explode the weapon. A bell was ringing below-decks. Under Keith's feet men were bawling out in fright and confusion. He threw his hands over his ears.

Just then the ship faltered. She hesitated for a moment as though she had run into a submerged reef. Then her forward motion stopped so abruptly that the gunners were hurled to the deck. Keith fell, clutching at the rail. Spilled cargo crashed and tumbled. He realized that the torpedo had struck, though the sound had been scarcely louder than that of a door slammed.

But the *Trader* felt the shot in her vitals. A white-hot flash illuminated the whole ship, and a geyser of dirty water burst upward. With it, the midships section of the freighter began to rise, drawbridge-fashion.

She was broken in half, wrecked like an old bus at a railroad crossing. Sliding down the deck, Keith clutched at the rail. He saw the screaming gunners falling from the bow into the water.

The second torpedo slammed into the after section a few seconds later. In her agony, the old ship seemed to cry out. Clouds of smoke and steam billowed up. An angry column of flame erupted from the forward cargo well. Trapped seamen screamed. The sound was so terrible that Keith panted in dumb agony for them.

And now the bow and stern separated and began sliding back into the ocean. There had been no life-boat drill. Nor was there really anything to do but to get off the ship by whatever means possible. He pulled off his shoes and straightened up. Then he saw that the water was covered with burning oil from the freighter's ruptured fuel tanks. As it burned, it made a frying sound; smoke and steam rose in sulphurous clouds.

He turned in panic to cross to the other side of the ship, but the deckplates had begun to glow cherry-red, like a stovelid. Now that there was no choice, he became calm. A line from the Psalms came to him.

"The Lord is my shepherd. . . ."

It was all he could remember of the verse. He climbed the rail, set himself carefully, and dived, covering his face as the flames engulfed him. He flashed through them so quickly that he scarcely felt their heat. The water closed upon him with its cold silence. He dived deep and started swimming.

3

He swam until the pain in his lungs was unbearable. Through the water came the sounds of the dying ship—breaking-up noises, explosions, loud screechings and rattlings. He surfaced, gasping, and looked back.

The fire was burning out in a collection of small, sooty bonfires. With a last churning uprush of steam and smoke, the stern section plunged from sight. Crates, spars, and wreckage bobbed on the water. A few survivors floundered in this oily flotsam. Only a jagged wall of steel remained of the ship's forward section.

The *Bataan Trader* sank wearily. It could not have been two minutes since she was struck by the first torpedo. She had been thirty years living, and two minutes dying.

Keith was not tired, but he knew he might be swimming for hours. He managed to remove his trousers. He rested and went back to work. After tying knots at the cuffs, he let the wind fill the trouser legs like wind socks. Then he twisted the top to keep the air from escaping, and found he could support himself by keeping hold of the inflated trousers.

Suddenly his heart gave a throb. He was sure he had heard the sound of an engine—a quiet *thrum-thrum-thrum*. He looked around, but there was nothing in sight. Yet he had faith in his hearing, if in nothing else right now, and on a sudden impulse he put his head under water and listened. There it was!

Thrum-thrum-thrum-thrum!

A motor of some kind was turning very quietly. And voices! He was positive he heard voices, somewhat like those ghost voices one heard, or *almost* heard, on a long-distance telephone line—voices just below the level of positive hearing.

Still nothing was in view, and he gave up looking for the fancied rescue boat.

As he rode the swells, he saw that the survivors on the scraps of flotsam were trying to paddle away from the lake of smoking oil. Then something obliterated them from his view—something black and dripping that rose to the surface like the back of a whale. He stared at it.

On the back of this monster there reposed a structure with the profile of a derby hat, from the crown of which a cluster of pencil-like tubes pointed upward.

It was several moments before he realized he was

looking at the submarine which had torpedoed the *Trader*.

Men were scrambling from the submarine onto her decks. He heard orders shouted in an Oriental tongue. The hard, white cylinder of a searchlight drilled through the smoke and steam, sweeping back and forth over the wreckage. Briefly it illuminated a swimmer Keith had not seen before; it started to pass on, but returned.

He heard a sharp popping sound. Little jets of flame flashed from the bridge of the submarine. Around the swimmer, whose white face was like a bull's-eye in the circle of light, small spurts of water geysered up. He threw his arm high, cried out, and sank from sight.

The searchlight whipped away, nosing greedily through the wreckage. The machine gun chattered again.

Keith started to swim toward the wounded man; then he stopped, for the man was already gone from sight. Numbed and sick, he gazed at the black fish shape. He was horrified, as though he had seen a child run over by an automobile. Anger came then, anger that wanted a gun to fire, a spear to hurl, a rock to throw. He could see the men crowded on the bridge of the sub. One man was operating the searchlight, another held a submachine gun; a third was peering at the water through binoculars.

The searchlight stopped again, but the quarry was hidden by the submarine itself. Keith heard a man shouting.

"You filthy heathen! You scum of the sea! You ——!" It sounded like Mister Mackenzie's voice.

Again the machine gun set up its uneven stuttering. The firing broke off and the searchlight moved on. As the misty beam swung toward him, Keith let the air out of his float and submerged. When he surfaced, the men on the sub were leaving the bridge. He heard metal clank, a grind of machinery came through the water, and a moment afterward the submarine began to move away.

He thought of that kindly man, Mister Mackenzie, with a twist of grief in his heart. But then, with an old boarding-house trick he had learned, he put the thought quickly out of his mind. Unhappiness, Keith had learned, was as weakening as hard physical labor, taking the strength right out of you.

He reinflated the trousers, lay on his back, and filled his mind with the beauty of a sky that was beginning to flush apricot with dawn. Seabirds glided above him, crying harshly and dipping low to see whether he was a suitable bit of flotsam to rest on. He did not want to reflect that of all the men who had left Honolulu yesterday morning on the *Bataan Trader*, he was the only one still alive.

4

Keith sat on a hatch cover he had found floating in the wreckage, and tried to get the oil out of his eyes. He was dizzy and seasick. The black muck covered him with a filthy but protective coating, and the oil in his eyes made his vision fuzzy. His short blond hair was matted to his skull. His face was streaked. The sun was growing hot.

Like most people, he had wondered what it would be like to be shipwrecked. He found it was such an enormous experience that it numbed him. His only resources, he suddenly realized, were in himself. He could not be sparing with water, because he had none. Having no food, he could not eat carefully. He could not fish, nor could he collect rainwater. His body and mind were his only survival kit.

On the hatch cover, he laid out his possessions.

One pocketknife; a sodden wallet full of cards and paper money; a handkerchief; some coins; and a small, flat piece of abalone shell. The rubbing of sand and water had worked the shell into the shape of an artist's palette. Pearly greens and pinks were revealed when one turned it. He had drilled a hole for a keychain, but the shell had no real purpose except to call up pleasant pictures and memories.

When he held the abalone shell now, he thought of how far it was to the bottom of the sea—through how many hundreds of fathoms of water the wreckage of the *Bataan Trader* and her crew must have sunk before they came to rest. He remembered the submarine, and for the first time in his life he could think pleasurably of killing. For the first time he was glad he was a good shot. A delicious picture formed in his mind of himself in the fork of a tree with a fine rifle in his hands, watching Japanese officers through a telescopic sight.

Suddenly there was a great, drenching roar of water that made him jump and look around. A shark-like prow had shot from the sea. Sunlight burned on wet highlights in a black, dented hull. Patches of white disfigured the plates. As the prow rose higher, a conning tower and foredeck followed. Green and white water foamed back in a torrent. The ship leveled off but kept rising, foam streaming from a line of freeing ports along the hull.

Keith climbed cautiously to his feet. In a futile but meaningful gesture, he opened the pocketknife. Hatch covers banged open. Men appeared on the bridge. They were Americans, and they were shouting at him. One of them trained a pair of binoculars on him as the submarine began to move closer. *"All stop!"* a man on the bridge called. *"Get a line to that man!"*

The sub came to a rocking halt. A sailor in a life jacket ran out on the foredeck and heaved him a line. It fell short, but Keith immediately dived in and swam toward it.

Several of the submarine sailors escorted him to a compartment in the after portion of the boat, and buckets of warm, soapy water were carried in. Standing on duckboards, he scrubbed himself industriously. He was so tired he could scarcely stay on his feet. The seawater had transformed the fuel oil to black taffy. Crewmen kept coming to grin at him and shake hands. Many of them were fairly young, but nearly all wore beards. The beards of the younger ones were so silky they reminded him of pictures of Jesus. All the men had a sunken-eyed, famished look. He learned later that they had just been on a long patrol during which they had nearly run out of food.

Weariness began to settle upon him like a weight. Drying slowly, he pulled on a pair of shorts. A big, farmerish man in a white skivvy shirt and greasy denims had supervised the cleaning operation. His name was McCord. He was the chief torpedoman, and someone said he was the "Chief of the Boat."

"Howya feelin' now?" he asked.

"Dead," Keith said, with a weak grin. "They bury livelier corpses than me."

"Rig a bunk for this boy," the chief said to a crewman.

"Crew's quarters, Chief?"

"That's all right."

McCord asked some questions about the sinking of the *Bataan Trader,* and Keith told him all he knew.

Wearing only the shorts, Keith followed the crewman through the submarine. From first to last, his main impression was one of crowdedness. Nowhere could two men pass abreast; nowhere could you take a deep breath without almost breaking a rib on something. Bulkheads and overheads were completely obscured by pipes, wiring, valves, and switch panels. It was not like being in a long, slim undersea boat; it was more like crawling through the heart of a gigantic alarm clock, where wheels and rods blocked you whichever way you turned. The machinery had come first; that it should be inhabited by human beings appeared to be an afterthought.

But the bed—he understood that. It was hard and narrow and it looked wonderful. He crawled onto it gratefully. Before he had drawn five breaths, he was asleep.

5

The captain of the submarine was a swarthy, serious man named Gaynor. When he heard that Keith was awake, he sent Chief McCord to bring him to the wardroom, a compartment about five by ten feet where the officers ate and did their paperwork. Clocklike instruments covered the bulkheads, and here and there a card was taped up showing the silhouette of a Japanese ship.

A mess attendant brought Keith a small, tender steak and mashed potatoes. He was too nauseated to enjoy the food.

"Steak all right?" the captain asked.

"It's fine, sir. I'm not very hungry."

"Eat what you want. Do you mind answering some questions?"

"Go ahead, Captain."

"Did you get a good look at this sub?"

"No, sir. It was just a silhouette. About all I could see were a lot of pipes sticking up out of the conning tower."

"Any particular shape to these pipes?"

"No. At least I didn't notice."

Captain Gaynor made notes. Though he was only in his thirties, his head was nearly bald and his remaining hair grew in the shape of a garland. He wore a suntan shirt and trousers, but nothing to denote his rank. A gold dolphin was pinned to his pocket.

"Did you see anything of the track of this torpedo before it hit?"

"Yes, sir. It was phosphorescent."

"Was there any steam or foam?"

"I didn't see any."

From the doorway, Chief McCord interrupted. "See any numbers on this sub?"

"No, sir. But it was big—bigger than this one."

"I-boat," said the chief positively.

Keith asked how they had known the freighter had been torpedoed. "A plane spotted the fire and sent out a call," the captain said. He looked at Keith appraisingly. "You don't seem to be much the worse for wear, young fellow. Anything you'd like that we can get for you?"

"Just one thing—"

"What's that?"

"A machine gun. And the crew of a Japanese submarine lined up against a wall."

"Oh, we do much better than that," the skipper said. "We've been known to put three or four fish into a destroyer and send it down with several hundred crewmen. And you should see what we can do with a gasoline tanker!"

"Are we heading back to Pearl Harbor now?" asked Keith.

"No, sir! We're heading for the barn—San Diego! This old wreck's taken her share of punishment. Now she gets some body and fender work, plus a few gadgets they've invented since she went on patrol."

The captain told Chief McCord to find Keith a place to bunk. Keith followed him down a narrow passageway with a green linoleum floor and smooth walls. It made him think of the aisle in a pullman, except that there were no windows.

They stepped over the high sill of an oval-shaped door and entered the next compartment. As soon as Keith looked into it, he knew this was the end of the line. There was no door in the far wall. The wall—bulkhead, they called it—looked as though a mad inventor had been granted indulgence to do anything he wanted with it. What he had done was to set six huge tubes into it in two vertical lines, each tube two feet across, with a manhole for a lid. These tubes were festooned with pipes, rods, wheels, gauges, and levers.

Along either side of the compartment were racks of torpedoes twenty feet long and nearly two feet thick. Above each torpedo was a bunk resembling a narrow trampoline. Seamen were sleeping on several of the bunks.

"Forward torpedo room," the chief muttered. "The things lying on the bunks are torpedomen. Now, this," he said, reaching out to smash his hand down on a torpedo, "is where you'll bunk."

Keith flinched as the meaty hand slapped the torpedo. He remembered how the freighter had stumbled, leaped into the air, and fallen back with her spine broken when one of those warfish had struck her. The chief chuckled.

"Don't worry about it going off. We couldn't explode one if we tried. Right, Henry?"

A boy lying on a bottom bunk spoke without opening his eyes. "Thaz right, Chief. That is so right."

"I mean we've stuck our periscope into places where a barracuda wouldn't be seen dead! We found the targets, and we banged it to 'em."

"How many did you sink?"

"Tell him, Henry."

"None," yawned Henry.

"None!" Keith echoed.

"Zeero, zeero—spelled none!" exclaimed the chief. "The brutes wouldn't go off. Sometimes they ran deep, sometimes they prematured. And *one* of them fish took off in a circle and nearly hit us coming around!"

"What's the matter with them?"

"The matter is they've got hot and cold running water, red lights and siren, and every other luxury you can think of. They're so complicated the instruction manual comes in three volumes. Maybe the old Mark X torpedo was built like an alarm clock, but at least if you hit anything with it, it went off!"

"Uh, Chief," Henry murmured, stirring restlessly. "Hadn't you better get some rest? You're off watch, aincha?"

"Sorry if I'm disturbing your sleep," the chief said huffily. "Stocker, this is Brockman. You'll meet the rest of the torps when they're awake."

Henry opened his eyes for as long as it took to shake hands. "Welcome aboard," he said.

Keith was surprised to find himself yawning again so soon after sleeping. He closed his eyes and felt the slight roll of the ship. Poised between sleeping and waking, he lazily turned thoughts over like stones in a tide pool. The moment you entered a place, you could sense whether the people in it liked each other. At some of the schools where he had boarded, there was irritation and unfriendliness; at others fun and good feeling.

There wasn't exactly fun in this submarine. But there was good feeling.

He dozed, but woke suddenly bathed in perspiration. Terror sat on his chest like a stone. A shout—his own—clanged about the iron cell. It was dark except for a night light, and in the warm dusk the torpedoman named Henry was standing on his bunk to shake Keith's shoulder.

"Hey, boy! Take it easy, huh?"

Keith thrashed over on his side and wildly stared about. From other bunks, men watched him. A moment before a torpedo had struck the submarine. Ripped open like a tin can by a firecracker, she had expelled all her precious air in one pained bellow and drunk in tons of green seawater. Her fuel oil had spread over the water and caught fire. It was like the *Bataan Trader* all over again.

He sank back on the bunk, panting. "I thought we'd been torpedoed!"

"I thought so, too, when I heard you yelling," Henry drawled. "Want me to get you a sleeping pill from the pharmacist's mate?"

"No, thanks."

Henry patted his shoulder. "Just scream if you need anything," he said with a grin.

6

In the short time it took the U.S.S. *Broadbill* to
reach San Diego, Keith discovered that there was
something mysterious about the men who went to
sea in submarines. Probably they were no tougher
nor more courageous than sailors anywhere else;
but they belonged more to the silent depths of the
ocean than to the treacherous water at its surface.

They used the ocean as fliers used the sky—used
its depth as well as its length and breadth. So they
were interested in the type of bottom below them
and the temperature of the water they floated in,
as well as the types and abundance of marine life,
for these factors had much to do with the submarine's safe operation. They took her three hundred
feet below the surface with complete confidence,
but they knew a single error on anyone's part would
send her down to the crushing blackness from which
no submarine ever rose.

He was surprised at the personal loyalty of the
men for their ship. A successful war patrol was *her*

success, not theirs. They pushed the buttons, but *she* performed the feats. She had her moods and quirks. The only man who could control these quirks was the captain, and because of his skill they accorded him the same sort of loyalty they gave the boat.

By the same token, however, they called all other boats "he." "He started a run on us, and we put two fish into him."

They realized that their real adversary was the enemy ship's commander, and the ship was exactly as dangerous as he was skillful.

Keith read old magazines and played cards with crewmen who were off watch. They were friendly, but he sensed that they held something back from him. Somehow they made him think of cowboys—independent, matter-of-fact, aware of being on their own. As he got to know them better, he liked them more, and an idea began to grow in him. It grew steadily, until one day he said to Chief McCord:

"How can I get permission to talk to the captain, Chief?"

McCord, who was making up a duty chart, picked up a sound-powered telephone. "Cap'm, control."

The handset rattled back: "Cap'm, aye."

"McCord, Cap'm. Our landlubber requests permission to speak to you."

"Granted," the captain said.

"He's in his quarters," McCord said.

The captain's cabin resembled a "roomette" on a train—a curtained cell with a bunk against the wall, plus a desk and a few square feet of space in which to move around. Instruments set in the wall enabled him to know at a glance the ship's course, the time, and various other matters relating to safety. When Keith knocked, Captain Gaynor told him to come in and sit on the bunk while he finished a letter.

"There!" he said, presently, with a grim edge to his voice. "For all the good it will do, I've just gone on record as being opposed to the kind of torpedoes they've been giving us to fire. Takes it out of you, Stocker, running the risks we do, only to have our weapons fail us. Oh, well!" he said ironically. "That's why they put an ice-cream freezer aboard a sub— to keep up morale. We're really very happy. We've been to the Orient and seen the world through a periscope. Wouldn't you like to join the submarine service?"

"Yes, sir!" Keith replied.

"Good, I'll swear you in right now."

"I'm serious! I've got to join some service pretty soon, and I think I'd like to be in a sub."

The captain stared at him. "I'll be darned if you aren't serious! How come you don't want to be a fighter pilot, like most kids your age?"

"It's kind of hard to say, Captain." Actually it was

not so much hard to say, as it was embarrassing to say it. The feeling he had was that all the submariners were members of a family, and the sub was their home. Everything that happened to it affected all of them. Some deep, strong feeling about the boat held them together. It was a feeling he had not known since his mother's death.

"Well, I guess it's the feeling of teamwork on the boat," he said, finally.

"There's that, all right. Either a sub's got teamwork, or it's got a crew breathing salt water. Do you know anything about the Navy?"

"Not much, but I love the sea. And I've done some goggle-fishing, and—"

"Do you like to hunt?"

Keith's glance dropped. "No, sir."

"Why not?"

"Well—" Keith scratched his neck. "I don't see much point in a sport where one side has all the advantage. Quail-hunting always seemed to me about like the Chicago Bears playing a junior high-school team."

The captain looked puzzled. "Not that there's anything wrong with hunting," Keith added quickly. "I mean, I'm not a vegetarian or anything. Only it seems to me that it's wrong to hunt if you *feel* that it's wrong."

"Do you know what submariners do?" asked the captain.

Keith looked at him, puzzled. "Sir?"

"We hunt. We hunt ships the way hunters hunt deer. We look for their smoke and listen for the sound of their heartbeat—the throb of their propellers. When we find a ship, we start taking bearings on it and get the torpedoes ready. We're practically panting with eagerness. We plan where we're going to hit him: right in the gut, where the boilers are. We're going to stop that heartbeat, see? There isn't a sound in the conning tower while we stalk him. But the minute we hear the torpedo hit, we go crazy! We know we've killed several hundred Japanese sailors, but we love it."

He leaned back and gazed closely at Keith. "If you don't like killing quail," he said, "how are you going to feel about killing men?"

Keith's blue eyes were steady. "I'd rather hunt quail," he said, "than be one. The other night I was the only quail that came off the *Bataan Trader* alive."

"Spoken like a true meat-eater." The captain laughed. "What about your folks? Would they give you a letter permitting you to join? You must be below age."

"My parents are both dead. But I think I could get a letter from my aunt and uncle. They're my guardians."

"I don't suppose your father was Navy? That might cut some red tape."

"No, sir. He was an Army officer."

Captain Gaynor smiled. "Well, assuming your health is satisfactory, et cetera, you're still supposed to do six months in the Navy before you can even apply."

Keith's mouth turned down. "Oh. Well, what if I scored high in my tests, something like that?"

"You've got two things working for you," the skipper said thoughtfully. "First, you're the orphan of an officer. Second, I know a lieutenant commander who'll give you a letter of recommendation."

"Who is that?"

"Me. I like the way you came through that torpedoing. If the flotilla commander endorses my letter, I don't see why you couldn't go to sub school right after boot camp. Especially since the boats are beginning to come off the production line faster than we can man them with qualified crews. I'll give you some advice, though: don't write any checks on your hopes."

7

From the sub tender anchored in San Diego harbor, Keith called his aunt and uncle in Los Angeles.

The *Broadbill* was safely in the "nest" of submarines moored beside the tender, a huge ship which was a floating machine shop, supply house, emergency hospital, and headquarters. Captain Gaynor had talked with the flotilla commander while his men took launches to the dock, to scatter across the country on leave. Keith was still standing in line before one of the telephone booths on the tender when the captain left by launch.

His aunt came on the line. When she recognized Keith's voice, she broke down. His uncle took over.

"Lord, boy, we thought you were gone till we got the Navy's telegram a couple days ago! Are you all right?"

"I'm fine, Uncle Hal."

"Well, thank heaven! I'll drive down tonight and pick you up."

"Okay. Er, Uncle Hal—"

"Here's your aunt, son! She wants to say hello now. You really shook her up!"

Aunt Julia, under fair control, said God had answered their prayers, and she would make a cake but it wouldn't be very good because she couldn't buy real butter any more, and tomorrow they would go shopping for new clothes for him.

"At least we can still buy clothes without too much trouble. But you should see the line when a store advertises mayonnaise, or cleaning tissues, or shortening. And *gasoline!* It's rationed now. Uncle Hal has a C card or he wouldn't even be able to drive down for you. Oh, I know we shouldn't complain, because others are suffering, too. But I just hope the armed forces are getting all those things, and not some politician in Washington."

As her voice went on, rich with self-pity, Keith realized that he was older, in some ways, than his aunt would ever be. Maybe you had to be torpedoed and machine-gunned to be able to put mayonnaise into its proper perspective.

While the monologue continued, he thought about First Mate Mackenzie of the *Bataan Trader*. How nobly his voice had challenged that sub captain! *"You heathen! You scum of the sea!"* He had stood up to them, and then died like a man and a sailor.

He wondered how his father had died, and whether he would ever have a letter from a chaplain or someone telling about it.

"I'm going into the Navy, Aunt Julia," he said, when she stopped for breath.

"What, dear?"

"I'm going into the Navy."

"The *Navy!* Oh, no!"

"Well, if I don't enlist in the Navy, the Army will get me next September. Or the Marines."

The word "Marines" shook her. She considered Marines as unhygienic and profane a group of men as it was possible to find since the passing of the pirates.

"But my darling, you're only a child!"

"They're taking children, though, Aunt Julia. So this child had better do it while he can."

A sigh. "Do you need a letter from us?"

"Yes, ma'am. I'm a little under age."

He could see her looking at the moss-smooth carpet and the shining kitchen; at the clean bath towel on the floor on which he was always forgetting to wipe his feet when he visited them. They had no children of their own, and he knew his visits were always a trial for them.

"Well, I suppose if it has to be done, there's no use fighting it. We'd have loved to have you with us, though, dear."

"I know. Tell Uncle Hal good-bye for me, will you?"

"Yes, dear. I'll pray for you every day."

8

Keith's naval career started at the Naval Training Center in San Diego, a collection of tall stucco barracks on the north shore of a beautiful bay. The adjustment to military life was not hard; the training was. He and his mates lost sleep and grew thin.

He wrote his aunt, once: "Thanks for the toll-house cookies, Aunt Julia. They were swell. They say the beds are swell here, too. I don't know, because I haven't been in one yet."

In a purgatory of fatigue and study, he learned a little bit about a great many things: fire-fighting, gunnery, compass reading, standing a watch. When it was over, the boots were jacks-of-all-trades, masters of none. But now they would ship out to various service schools for training in a specialty. He waited a week, while long lists of trainees departed. At last his name came up.

The truck took him to the depot, where he met a Mexican boy named Hector Rubio who would travel with him. Rubio was going to the submarine school at New London, Connecticut, from a destroyer, and having a modest rating he was in charge of the two-man troop movement. He was a stocky fellow with wide jaws, bright black eyes, and a fine smile. Scars marred his eyebrows and the bridge of his nose. Keith, who had boxed in school, recognized them as scars of bare-fist combat.

"Just show proper respect for your superiors," Hector said with a grin, "and we'll get along fine."

For two weeks they traveled slowly east, transferring and retransferring. Hector had been on a ship which was bombed at Pearl Harbor. Keith asked why he had put in for subs.

"Playing the odds," Hector confided. "The only ships that didn't take a beating at Pearl Harbor were subs. How can they hurt a ship that's *supposed* to sink? So I transferred."

Later he said, "I was a Mexican citizen until a year ago. Then I joined up to get U.S. citizenship."

"What for?"

"To make money! What else? Money for Citizen Rubio."

Keith had expected some high-sounding declaration—a blossom of virtue plucked from the Gettysburg Address. "At least you're honest," he laughed.

"Why kid myself, Stock? Who's going to take care of a man if he don't take care of himself? I was fightin' on the streets of Tijuana when I was ten years old. Everybody was hungry. I said to myself,

This is just a *carcel sin barras,* a jail without bars. I'm going to get out of it."

"I'm glad you did, Hec."

"Plus, I made a hundred and sixty-three dollars my last month on the *McKnight. In addition to* my salary!"

"No kidding!"

"Poker," explained Hector. "These swabbies will bet a month's salary on anything."

"It's still luck, though. And when it changes you'll lose that hundred and sixty-three, *in addition to* your salary."

"Luck is no part of it," Hector scoffed. "It's how the other guys look and act when they play. In a half-hour, I know more about them than their own mothers do."

At last, one night, the train rolled into New London and came to a shuddering stop. They stepped onto a wooden platform. A light rain was falling, as fine as salt. At the base they drew bunks in a two-story barracks and slept like dead men. Two days later their training began. In a short time neither could remember what idleness had been like.

9

A submarine candidate was a shovelful of crude ore from which a fine grade of steel was going to be smelted. This ore must be studied carefully before being reduced to the molten state for processing. Physicians searched the candidates' bodies for flaws. Men who passed their physical examinations then entered a pressure chamber, where their ears and sinuses were subjected to fifty-pound jolts of air pressure. Decayed teeth began to ache; faulty ears shrieked in protest. More men were disqualified.

In a silolike water tower, the trainees swam from a depth of one hundred feet to the surface. Any who panicked during this simulated escape from a wrecked submarine were quietly shipped back to duty. Psychologists ran tests to weed out men who had too much imagination to endure submarine life; men who quarreled readily, were not personally clean, or got bored quickly.

Now the ore was reduced to iron. Some of this iron would become steel, some would crack under the intensive formal instruction.

Instruction started with the examination of a model submarine. Keith learned that a submarine was almost as big as a destroyer, but that most of it consisted of tanks enclosing a small, airtight "pressure hull." These tanks could be flooded with seawater to submerge the ship, or filled with fuel to run the four big diesel engines.

The theory of submerging and surfacing was simple. Suppose you inserted a cork in the neck of an empty bottle, the instructor explained, and placed the bottle in water. It would float. Remove the cork; it would fill and sink. But permit only a certain amount of water to enter the bottle before restoppering it, and it would reach a state of "neutral buoyancy." Push it under; it would neither sink nor rise. Its weight would be exactly that of the water it displaced.

This was how a submarine operated. Enough water was let into her buoyancy tanks to place her in neutral buoyancy. Then the fins at her bow and stern, called planes, could be used to maneuver her like a fish.

What made the process complicated was that the ship kept changing weight, so that more or less water had to be taken in. As the diesel oil was burned, the ship became lighter. Seawater had to be let into the emptying fuel tanks constantly to compensate for this loss in weight. Each torpedo fired lightened her by hundreds of pounds. A salvo of four shots from the bow torpedo tubes immediately lightened the bow by over a thousand pounds! It was up to the diving officer to see that the ship did not "broach" —pop out of the water like a cork, so that her intended victims would see her and open fire.

After this preliminary instruction, the training company was split up into twelve-man "diving sections" and marched to the docks. A diving section was the smallest number of men who could take a sub out and bring it back. Standing there in the gray morning, they smiled at the archaic "O-boats" in which they were going to train. Dating from 1915, the subs were half the length of a modern boat. Instead of a sleek conning tower, they displayed a battered structure like a tomato can athwart a narrow deck.

"I've seen bigger boats in toy stores," Rubio said. "What's it run on—carbide and water?"

"Rubber bands," Keith said. "They just wind up the propeller and turn us loose."

But the old O-boat did her job, within the limits of the trainees' ability. She dived too steeply and surfaced sluggishly, and her dummy torpedoes went astray; but she cruised back up the Thames River in the evenings wet and proud.

After a week of becoming acquainted with the ship, the trainees returned to the classrooms. Keith soon found himself struggling desperately to keep up. Math and engineering were hard for him. Electricity was baffling. He liked sonar—identifying ocean sounds picked up on the sub's sensitive sound gear, her "ears." He had an aptitude for it, and his hearing was acute. But it was over quickly and now they were into the mystery of the torpedo.

A veteran torpedoman named Herb Jolley was the assistant torpedo instructor. Scuttlebutt was that Chief Jolley had once been fleet heavyweight. Keith believed the story, for Jolley certainly looked like an old pug, with his broken nose, cauliflower ears, and crew-cut hair. His bullet head was set deeply into his shoulders and heavy pads of cartilage overhung his eyes.

On the first day of instruction, he abruptly stabbed his pointer at Keith.

"What's your name, sailor?"

"Stocker. Keith T."

"Who'd you vote for in the last election?"

"I'm not old enough to vote, Chief."

"And that goes for at least half the men in this class! Some of you probably don't have to shave more'n once a week. But in a few weeks you'll be heading for action. And where does the Navy put the men who know the boats? In training schools!"

The class sat stiffly while he finished sounding off. They were baffled, but clearly aware that Jolley was smarting under some fancied injustice.

"I wouldn't be shore-based five minutes, if I could

get sea duty," he told them bitterly. "I can go on any sub blindfolded and name you every control I touch! That's the way we learned the boats in the old Navy. And that's the way I teach torpedoes. I'm not teaching young men to sail model boats: I'm teaching them to seek and destroy the enemy. Is that clear?"

Everyone nodded vigorously.

The chief's gaze came back to Keith. "Stocker, what are you striking for?"

"Sonarman."

Jolley's face reddened. "Nobody strikes for a specialty until he finishes here. If you bilge out, you're not striking for anything. What makes you think you'd make a good ping jockey?"

Keith supposed the chief had picked him for a target because he was younger than the others. "I don't know."

"Sound off! You must have had some reason. Maybe you fancy yourself in headphones, eh? The boy sonarman of the silent service!" The class laughed, and Jolley grinned and went on.

"I can see it now! You're sitting at the sonar stack cranking the soundhead around. The captain stands behind you, waiting for the word. The safety of the ship depends on you. You could hear a pin drop in the conning tower. Suddenly you've got it! 'Destroyer sounds at two five zero, sir!' you report.

'Belay that,' the captain says. 'That's your own bubble gum you've been listening to.' "

The classroom rang with laughter. Keith kept his eyes down. To look into Jolley's battered, arrogant face might release the anger he was trying to hold in. Satisfied, Jolley strolled to a huge, cutaway torpedo on its rack and laid a hand on its steel shell. As he began to speak, Keith whispered to Hector:

"Man! He's got the disposition of a bulldog with corns!"

"Stocker!" Jolley whirled from the torpedo.

Keith jerked like a puppet. "I hear you, Chief!"

"On your feet!"

Jolley walked toward him. Keith stood ramrod-straight, thumbs along trouser creases, chin tucked in.

"What did you say?"

"I—I said you had a temper."

The chief put his face close to Keith's. He was four inches taller, with the look of a heavy cruiser —a slow, brawling, physical man. But there was a hard brightness of intelligence behind his eyes.

"Do you think I've been picking on you?" he asked.

"I—I don't know."

"You bet I have. Because I don't like trainees that come from boot camp on a free-ride basis."

"Sir?"

"I mean men with a letter from a two-starrer certifying them for sub training."

"Oh." Keith flushed.

"How *was* the admiral when you saw him last?"

"It wasn't an admiral. It was the captain of a submarine."

"Okay. Now lemme tell you something. Maybe you better have it tattooed on your lip where you'll see it every time you shave: you got here easy, but you'll get out hard. Understand?"

"Yes." Keith stared at a point on his forehead until the chief grunted, "Carry on," and walked back to the torpedo.

10

"*Stocker, you're at Position A and the ship you're attacking is at B. What is your true target bearing?*"

"*The true target bearing, Chief, is the angle between the, uh, fore-and-aft axis of your own ship and the, uh, line of—*"

"*As you were! That's your relative bearing.*"

"*Stocker, what is this mechanism?*"
"*Sir, that's the, uh—blow and vent manifold.*"
"*This is the gyro setting indicator regulator!*"

"*Water is reported in the after battery compartment, Stocker. What do you do?*"

"*You isolate the compartment and force the water out with your 225-pound system.*"

"*What about your electrician's mate? Going to leave him in the battery compartment and force him out, too?*" (Laughter.)

But other men were having trouble, also, for there was more than anyone could absorb. The theory of submarine security was that every man must be qualified to fill any job on the boat. These were the last of the corsairs, far-raiding buccaneers who depended absolutely on their own adroitness to get them back.

Finally specialty ratings were announced. To his surprise and alarm, Keith was posted as a torpedoman apprentice.

He thought in numb desperation, *Jolley did it! He knows I'll bilge out.* He walked to company headquarters and requested permission to speak to the chief yeoman.

"Is the notice on the bulletin board right, Chief? I thought maybe I was up for sonar. I got my best grades there."

The chief rubbed his cigar ash off on a tin can lid. He was a red-faced, corpulent man with a voice like burlap. "Life is full of little surprises, Stocker. What else is on your mind?"

"Who teaches the class?"

The yeoman glanced at an onionskin paper in a basket. "Lieutenant Martin has a class in gunnery and torpedo. Let's see, though. . . . You're in Chief Jolley's section." He puffed on the chocolate-brown cigar. "And just between us swabbies, you've got the best instructor at the school. He was firing torpedoes when you were still paddling around in waterwings."

"I know."

"He made up his list himself, so I guess you made quite an impression on him. Gee, I wish I was you, Stocker."

"So do I."

Keith walked out. These old chiefs hung together like the last human beings in a world full of cockroaches. They went on liberty together, came back together, lowered their voices when a trainee was within a hundred yards, and kept the galley help up till midnight bringing coffee when they held a scuttlebutt session.

Jolley opened the advanced torpedo class with a lyrical tribute to the torpedo. It was embarrassing to listen to him. He sounded like a poet praising a beautiful woman with whom he was hopelessly in love. While he eulogized the Mark XIV, Keith doodled disgustedly in his notebook.

"A ton and a half of man's finest workmanship," Jolley declared. "One of these little darlings, costing a mere ten thousand dollars, will sink a battleship costing millions! Instruct her right, and she'll run straight, hot, and normal. If you miss, don't blame the fish—blame yourselves."

Keith glanced up, shocked. Didn't he know the new torpedoes were being cursed all over the Atlantic and the Pacific?

"I'm going to teach you how to keep the Mark XIV in service, and then we're going out with the new officers and practice till you and they can hit a barracuda on sonar bearings. And don't write me any postcards saying you hit a ship and the fish didn't explode! Because these babies are built with jeweler's tools and armed with a half-ton of TNT!"

Keith's arm rose, almost of its own volition. Jolley acknowledged him with a nod. "Uh, Chief—is that the Mark XIV?"

"That's my baby."

"I heard from a submarine skipper that there were a few duds. Is that right?"

Jolley stood straighter, faintly smiling. A small cloud of suspicion blew across Keith's mind. Had Jolley been putting out bait that he had taken?

"What did your skipper friend say about the Mark XIV, Stocker?" Jolley asked pleasantly.

"He told me they fired twenty-four fish on one patrol, and none of them ran true."

"I don't say there aren't any duds, Captain Stocker —excuse me, *Seaman* Stocker. All I say is that a skipper who wastes a whole load of torpedoes isn't instructing them right. Maybe this man had *maru* fever. Maybe when he saw a Jap *maru* steaming along, he'd break into a cold sweat and start throwing torpedoes like rocks."

Keith thought of the battered old *Broadbill* reeling home with dents in her hull and her crew gaunt from the long patrol. He knew he was outclassed; he should have known better than to argue torpe-

48

does with a torpedo instructor. But he owed his life to Captain Gaynor, and he respected his judgment.

"Maybe there's two kinds of war, Chief," he said. "Classroom war, and shooting war."

Jolley's jaw muscles ridged. "Get up," he snapped.

Keith rose, the backs of his legs pressing the chair. Jolley approached.

"I've been asking for sea duty for two years," Jolley said. "It's not like I was hiding here, you know."

"I know. I'm just saying—"

"You see," the chief interrupted, "the Navy makes all the decisions for us. That's why unqualified boots like you sometimes land here because they've got friends upstairs. And it's why a torp with seventeen years on him has to stay here teaching boots to wipe their noses."

A snicker from the trainees. Keith smiled. "They do say those aptitude tests will uncover a man's talents, Chief," he said.

Jolley's face darkened. Then his shoulder moved; that was all. But the room rocked out of focus, spun, and went dark. In a moment, Keith's vision cleared and he could see dark, oiled flooring beneath him. He was on his hands and knees. A drop of blood spattered the floor. His mouth and chin felt numb.

Someone was trying to help him up. He pushed him away and rose on his knees, staring at the chief.

Jolley stood there with his big, sloping shoulders sagging and his face congested with color.

"Get up!" he growled.

Keith got to his feet. His head was clear.

"Am I on report?"

Jolley's manner had changed. There was a shadow of guilt in his face. "No. Probably *I* am. Report to the duty officer that you were struck by a petty officer. . . . Well, go on!" he invited. "Do I have to pipe you out of the room?"

Keith rubbed his chin. "I suppose if I'd hit you first, it would have been all right? Is that it?"

"That's it," the chief said sourly.

Smack!

Jolley shuffled back a pace and put a hand to his cheek. He gazed in astonishment at the youngster who had just thrown a punch at him. There was a smear of blood on Keith's mouth, but he was beginning to grin.

"Oh. It's like that!" Jolley said, comprehending. "Now we're even, is that it? You don't report me if I don't report you."

"That's the idea."

Jolley pondered a moment. Then he grinned. "You got yourself a deal." Keith sat down and Jolley returned to his place. Coolly, he laid a hand on the cutaway torpedo and looked out over the class.

"We will now take up the matter of retracting the detonator. . . ."

11

Suddenly it was over.

Once again men were packing and getting their orders, saying good-bye, and roaring away in trucks, while men who had not been called sat around the depopulated barracks killing time. Some of the class was transferred to a submarine recently completed at the Electric Boat Works at nearby Groton. Others went to specialty schools for further training.

To everyone's surprise, Chief Jolley's name came up on a shipping order. After many attempts he had finally got sea duty. His orders sent him to a Navy airfield for retransfer by the earliest available transportation.

Three days passed, and none of Keith's diving section had been called. Then all the names appeared in a cluster on a list one morning. They boarded a train that night, and as it moved off with a preliminary thunder of couplings the petty officer in charge opened the sealed orders. He read the mimeographed sheet and looked up.

"Mare Island!"

"Where's 'at?" Rubio asked.

"San Francisco!" someone said. "Best liberty port in the world!"

"So what? We won't get liberty. They'll attach us to a new sub and send us right out on a shakedown cruise."

"Who says? We may go out on an old sugarboat."

"Naw, it'll be a new boat. Reconditioned, anyway."

"Yeah. One of them World War I retreads like we trained in!"

Keith sank into the worn plush seat, not caring much, just relaxing in the knowledge that he had made it. Despite Jolley, despite everything, he had not bilged out. Now he was part of the submarine war.

One night, a week later, they carried their seabags from the train and waited on a foggy siding. At last a truck appeared and they roared off through the Navy docks of Mare Island. The driver said they were going to a new boat.

"*Gato*-class," he said. "All the refinements."

"Such as what?"

"Satin lining throughout, and silver handles to carry it by. They say it's shaped just like a coffin."

"Aw, stow it!"

The driver laughed.

The truck stopped on a concrete ramp and they dismounted again. "There she is!" the driver said, pointing.

They turned and saw her, but no one said a word. Keith gave a shiver of excitement. He would never forget that first eerie impression, for in the darkness, without a light anywhere aboard, she was a long fishlike shape scarcely more tangible than night and mist—a ripple on the water, a silhouette that could be a trick of the eyes. Her upper surfaces were dark gray, sprinkled with highlights where the mist had settled. The coaming which enclosed the conning tower and bridge rose smoothly from the deck like a shark's dorsal fin. On the afterdeck was a four-inch gun. She looked cold, efficient, dangerous, and beautiful.

The truck roared away. Keith took a quick breath and glanced around at the others. They, too, were just coming out of the spell. Rubio took off his white cap in salute.

"Dollar gets you five she'll do twenty knots!" he breathed.

Carrying their seabags, they approached the railed brow which crossed to the deck. The petty officer in charge of the group looked around. "Where's the gangway watch?"

They gazed up and down the boat. "There isn't even a deck watch!" Keith said.

"What's to keep somebody from goin' aboard and stealing the deck gun?" asked Rubio.

"Well—we gonna stand here all night?" asked one of the men.

"What do Regulations say about going aboard without permission?" the petty officer said, uneasily.

Keith set down his heavy seabags. He was eager to see the inside of the boat, and quite willing to be the first aboard. "I'll go," he said.

He crossed the brow to the deck. Standing on the wooden slats, he felt the power and speed gathered in the tons of batteries below decks; in the sixty-four hundred horsepower of fine diesel engines.

"Hey!" he called. No reply. Going forward, he found the foredeck hatch closed. He climbed a ladder in the steel "sail" which enclosed the bridge, periscope shears, and cigarette deck. The cigarette deck was abaft the bridge, a little railed enclosure with a machine gun mounted in it. Everything had an immaculate newness, though a light crusting of salt showed that the boat had already been out on training runs. He slipped past the lookout's perch to the bridge. In the middle of the little steel crypt where the officers directed the boat on the surface were a compass and a mounted pair of pressure-proof binoculars.

Something moved at his feet. He jumped back. A blackout flashlight poured a blue light over him. "Who goes there?" a man growled. He wore a pea

54

jacket, dungarees, and a baseball cap. In addition to the flashlight he was holding a comic book.

"You the gangway watch?" asked Keith.

"Affirmative. Gunner's Mate Scobie. Why didn't you sing out?"

"Torpedoman Apprentice Stocker. I did. That must be a good story, Scobie."

Scobie chuckled. "I been trying for three days to find out how Superman's going to get out of that well they dumped him in. The Chief of the Boat's a fool for work and my reading's suffered bad. He's going to ruin my eyesight, making me read by flashlight. How many men with you?"

"Fifteen."

"Come on."

He ducked through the conning tower and dropped through the hatch. Keith leaned over the edge of the coaming. "Welcome aboard, men!" he called.

In the conning tower, Scobie checked them in on a clipboard. "Go on down to the control room and report to the duty officer." He climbed back to the bridge. They descended the ladder to the control room directly beneath the conning tower and reported to a lieutenant who was having a cup of coffee as he read a newspaper. The lieutenant looked them over and picked up a telephone.

"Chief Jolley to the control room."

Keith looked at Rubio, who began to laugh silently. "That wouldn't be *Herbert* Jolley, sir?" Keith asked the officer.

"Yes, it would. Do you know him?"

Keith sighed. "Yessir. We met in New London."

"Fine. Then you're used to his ways," said the lieutenant, with a smile which could mean anything.

Jolley assigned bunks. A few of the newcomers went to the after torpedo compartment, several joined the complement in the main crew's quarters, and the rest finished in the forward torpedo room. Keith drew one of the top bunks, where the heat collected, sharing the space with a torpedo. Jolley smiled up at him as he tried to get settled without slashing his scalp open on a valve.

"If you ask me, Stocker, it's the best bunk on the boat. Anytime you want toast, just lay a piece of bread on that resistor bank overhead. Don't electrocute yourself, though. I'll let you know when I want to inspect the torpedo, and you can move your gear."

"Fine, Chief. What's the name of this boat? The *Bounty*?"

"You'd think so, to hear the people cry about polishing brass. No, it's the *Mako*. Speaking of brass, there's a can of polish yonder. You might put some polish on Number One breech door. Work your way down to Six and I'll check your work."

Keith smiled and dropped to the deck. There

had been no spit and polish aboard the *Broadbill,* and he did not believe the *Mako*'s captain would stress it. Not if the gangway watch got away with reading comics. A big, black-browed man who bunked beneath him lowered a book he had been reading.

"I'll be glad when you run out of polish, Jolley. I ain't smelled so much since Lieutenant Ramage got his new collar bars."

"What's *Mako* mean?" Rubio asked.

"It's a shark," Keith said.

"Who's the captain?" someone asked.

"Casey, Louis G.," said the black-browed man. "Most of us haven't seen him yet, but the scuttlebutt is that he went right into Singapore harbor and blasted a Jap battleship out of the water. He's in Washington getting a Congressional Medal pinned on him right now."

"How do these stories get started?" Jolley scoffed. "Casey's got a helluva reputation in the pigboats, Hartman, but the medal is a Navy Cross, and it's for making tide tables off Guadalcanal so the invasion boats wouldn't get stranded."

"Who's the executive officer?" Keith asked.

"Hasn't reported. I hear he's in sick bay. The boat went through her shakedown cruise before Casey went on leave. Now I'm just waiting for him and the exec to show up."

"How much more time are you giving them before you put out to sea, Chief?" the big man named Hartman asked.

Jolley glowered at him and went aft. He did not answer, and Keith darted a respectful glance at Hartman, who closed one eye in a wink. He was about twenty-five, with the build of a lumberjack and a round head on which the hair had been clipped almost to the skull. His shoes and socks were off, and Keith could see a rooster tattooed on one foot and a pig on the other. He remembered an old superstition that such an arrangement was proof against drowning. He wondered how many hands on the *Bataan Trader* had worn a rooster and pig inside their shoes.

12

In the morning Jolley roamed the boat, looking for work to keep all hands occupied. Only the chief petty officers and a few old submarine hands like Hartman were safe from the Chief of the Boat's restless perfectionism. Hartman, a friendly bull of a man who was alternatively called Toro and The Beast Who Walks Like a Man, sensed Jolley's hostility to Keith and advised patience.

"If he was a horse," he said, "I'd say he'd gone barn-sour. A barn-sour horse has forgot how to act on the trail, and keeps lookin' back. Jolley thinks this boat is a training barracks. He knows submarines, though."

"What's going to change him?"

"The Old Man. A fightin' submariner like Casey knows that no amount of brass polish ever sank a ship. Just keep your shirt on, Sandblower."

"What's that mean?"

Hartman, six inches taller, patted him on the head. "Sandblower? It means Shorty."

For three days, polish rags snapped and the crew drilled. Then Captain Casey arrived. Like the Fourth of July. Like laughter. His voice boomed out over the main circuit to all compartments.

"Now, hear this! This is the captain. Secure whatever you're doing and fall in on the afterdeck on the double!"

It was the rich, supple voice of a man who could be tough one minute and laugh at a joke on himself the next. And since the world holds few voices and fewer men like that, every sailor on the *Mako*, including tall-water sailors like Chief Jolley, stood at attention until the circuit clicked off.

Throughout the boat there was a moment's paralysis; then a thudding of feet on the deck. Keith snatched his cap and ran to the escape trunk ladder. He scrambled up behind a pair of grease-stained Navy shoes and took his place on the afterdeck.

His arms crossed, Lieutenant Commander Casey watched his command take tangible form. He wore a tan gabardine uniform with battle ribbons and shoulder boards. The soft sunlight burned on his face and struck golden sparks from his dolphins. At his feet rested a small cardboard crate and a blue zipper bag.

The junior officers fell in near him. The last man up the hatch was Jolley, stuffing in a clean shirt as he came.

"Report!" shouted the acting executive officer.

"All hands present or accounted for, sir!" Jolley responded.

Captain Casey received the exec's report and let his gaze roam the group. There were faint pouches beneath his eyes, and his mouth was wide and flexible. He had a long chin, split by a small vertical line, and deep brackets beside his mouth. He looked athletic and supple, in the style of a tennis player.

"A lot of you men are new," he said, finally. "I'm afraid you won't be new long. One thing about submarines—they don't wait for the war to come to them. There's no noncombatants aboard a sub. We're going down to San Diego now, and go through some training exercises. The main idea is to get to know each other. It'll be about like New London, except that we'll carry a few fish with warheads—just in case.

"You may have heard that my old boat got a unit citation. Actually, we didn't have much choice. We had to earn a citation to come through alive. It boils down to the fact that to do any damage, you've got to go where the enemy shipping is. And in a short time that's where we're going to be."

He turned to the acting executive officer. "Mister Bratton, have I forgotten anything?"

"No, sir!"

"Has my executive officer shown up?"

"No, sir."

"How about my chief?"

"Yes, sir!" shouted Jolley, pulling his stomach in.

"Very well. I've heard good things about you, Chief. I'm sure you'll take in stride the first assignment I'm going to give you." He nudged the crate at his feet. "We've got a fine crew's mess on this boat, but it lacks one thing—a fireplace. Have this installed at once."

There was a roar of laughter. Casey waved his hand, picked up the zipper bag, and the formation was over. Jolley moved warily to the crate, and Keith heard him mutter: "A fireplace!"

13

Jolley and an electrician's mate installed the fireplace. It was a metal hearth about two feet square, with simulated logs and a red light which created an illusion of surging flames. Then they installed another of the captain's "comforts," a real porthole for the wardroom—except that on the glass there was a painting of a beach with palm trees, and girls sunning themselves.

Out where the water was purple, *Mako* dived and surfaced and dived again, frolicked like a porpoise and raced like a barracuda. Then she sank to two hundred feet and lay in the heavy water without a sound, rigged for silent running. Even the air conditioning was secured, and the humidity shot to maximum and the boat began to smell, according to Casey, like a fireman's socks.

Up on the surface again, she was lunging along through the big swells when Casey pressed the diving alarm. *"Clear the bridge! Dive, dive!"*

As the raucous *Ah-ooo-gah! Ah-ooo-gah!* of the

diving alarm penetrated the submarine, officers and men came tumbling into the conning tower from the bridge. The conning tower was a tiny, separate hull riding piggyback on the ship's main pressure hull. In essence, it was a duplicate of the control room, directly below it.

"Up periscope!"

The skipper crouched by the periscope well as the slim tube hummed up through the tower. Rising with it, he flipped the handles down and pressed his brow to the rubber buffer. A quartermaster closed the hatch and spun the wheel which dogged it tight. The throb of the diesels ceased. Air-breathers like the crew, the engines could not function underwater. The faint purr of electric motors started up.

In the control room, Chief Jolley stood before the hydraulic manifold, with Mister Bratton, the diving officer, at his shoulder. The chief was opening vents in the ballast tanks to admit water, as all outer hatches closed to keep water from entering the pressure hull. As each vent opened, a red light on the Christmas Tree—the warning panel before him—would become green.

As the last red light flickered out, he reported:

"Green board!"

Bratton called for compressed air and watched the barometer. "Pressure in the boat!" He tapped the depth gauge to loosen the needle. "Six-five feet, sir!"

"Very well. Blow negative to the mark." Casey checked the time. "Seventy seconds. We've got to do better than that. They can drop a lot of bombs on us in seventy seconds."

Later, *Mako* made rendezvous with a target ship.

In the torpedo rooms, the crews stood nervously at their stations. Keith mentally ran through the procedure, while Jolley stood between the banks of tubes.

"Fire Two!"

The solenoid clicked in Number Two tube, followed by a hiss, and the smashing impact of compressed air expelling the warfish. The boat bucked. Jolley reached up and pulled a valve. Water roared into the bilge to compensate for the loss in weight. Then the water was cut off with a trip-hammering shudder. In the sudden quiet, Keith turned his head to hear better. He was certain he had heard the faint whisper of the torpedo racing away. He pictured it shooting up from the green depths toward the sunlight, streaming bubbles. He thought of swimming beside the boat while the torpedoes raced out, and watching them disappear like sharks in the . . .

"*Stocker! Close the outer door!*"

Jolley's shout startled him. He came back from his daydream to leap for the big crank. He spun it, and reported:

65

"Number Two tube secured!"

Jolley shot him a look of disgust.

Between training sessions, the chief found plenty of work to keep the crew busy. Old hands who had been through the Philippine disaster began to grumble. Dials gleamed, stainless steel radiated a silver luster, the decks were spotless. When there was nothing left to clean, Jolley would distribute handbooks to study, such as *Meeting the Samoans*.

Keith found escape in a sonar manual. When the sonarman adjusted his headphones, he became the ears of the submarine, sifting the ocean's whispers and watchlike tickings. He must be able to differentiate between the rumblings of a sperm whale and the sound of an approaching warship. He must be able to calculate a destroyer's speed by counting the revolutions of its propellers.

Except for Jolley, he would probably be a first-rate sonarman instead of a nervous torpedoman.

One night Lieutenant Ramage, the torpedo and gunnery officer, called for a test of the tubes. Jolley turned out the torpedo crews fore and aft. To test a torpedo tube, an "inboard slug" was fired, which was no more than a blast of air which burst back into the compartment when the firing key was pressed. With the outer doors closed and the inner doors open, the compressed air which normally launched the torpedo merely blew back into the boat.

Waiting while the starboard tubes were tested, Keith daydreamed of a young sonarman sitting at the console during a battle approach. The captain was saying, "Radar, what's the range?"

"Blanked out by the rain, Captain!"

"Sound, what've you got?"

"Bearing, zero nine zero, Captain!"

"Speed?"

"Make it eleven knots, sir."

"Undog Number Two breech door," a voice said. Keith gave a start when he realized it was Lieutenant Ramage. Ramage and the chief had moved over to the port tube bank where Keith was waiting. He threw open the breech door. The bronze stern of a practice torpedo could be seen in the tube, dull gold and steel. Ramage grunted in displeasure, and Jolley muttered:

"Always crack the door before you open it. The outer door might be open."

"Charge Number Two air flask."

Keith pulled a valve. Compressed air sighed into the air flask.

"Fire Two."

Whoosh! A blast of air rushed into the compartment.

"Secure Two." Ramage checked a paper on his clipboard. "Undog Number Four."

Keith opened Number Four tube, charged the flask, and fired on order. There was no blast of air. The boat gave a peculiar shudder. Starting gears whined. He looked blankly at the torpedo officer, aware that something was wrong. The lieutenant quickly stepped forward and examined the pressure gauge.

At the same moment, Jolley saw what had happened and shoved Keith out of the way.

"*You fired Number Six!*" he shouted. "*Six is a warshot!*"

As Jolley attacked the firing gear, Lieutenant Ramage reported the disaster to the bridge by telephone. Keith stood where Jolley had shoved him. He felt the submarine tremble as her motors went into reverse. Jolley recharged the impulse flask for Number Six tube.

"Was the outer door open?" Ramage asked.

"No, sir! But the pressure gauge shows that it's open now."

"Can you tell whether the torpedo cleared it?"

"No, sir. I'm going to give her another shot of air and find out."

Keith pictured it weakly. Under certain conditions, a torpedo could explode close to the ship. The magnetic exploder would detonate in the presence of metal, such as a submarine hull. But before the half-ton of TNT in the warhead was "armed"—ready to explode—the torpedo had to travel at least 400 yards. To measure this distance, a little paddle wheel in the nose, coupled to the propeller of the torpedo, started turning as soon as the torpedo was fired. The torpedo did not have to leave the tube to be armed; once it was fired, the paddle wheel would continue to run.

Another pop of the firing valve, and the needle on Number Six tube wavered and slowly swung down to zero.

"She's stuck!" the chief panted. "The air leaks past her but won't throw her out."

"Try it again," Ramage ordered. As he picked up a phone to report to the bridge, Keith seized his arm.

"Permission to inspect the torpedo, sir! If the wheel's turning, maybe I can jam it."

"Go ahead, for God's sake! Take a screwdriver. I'll clear you with the bridge. Wait for clearance at the escape trunk."

Jolley pulled a screwdriver from a drawer and tossed it at him. Keith ripped off his shoes and ran for the escape hatch. In a moment Ramage shouted, "You're clear! Take off!" Keith shoved the heavy hatch open on an evening sky startlingly beautiful, a pale blue dome washing into orange at the horizon. Rocking slowly in the quiet sea, *Mako's* bow was outlined by a blue-green wake surging forward after her emergency stop. He ran from the slatted deck onto the bow plating, stopping about ten feet back from the bullnose.

He tried to estimate how far below the water line the tube would be. The tube was on the port side, and what daylight was left was streaming against that side of the ship. A geyser of steam and bubbles was rising from below. The ship began rising by the head. They were venting a group of tanks to bring the tubes closer to the surface.

He dived into the water and saw the dark bulges of the tube doors through the huge, silvery air pockets rising from Tube Six. Two and Four were closed. He came down to Six. The nose of the torpedo protruded like an ugly growth on the side of a fish. He ran his hands over it and felt the vibration of the steam-driven engine in its stern section. His groping fingers found nothing. He pressed his ear against it to listen, and heard a slight whirring sound under the steady grind of the engine. His heart gave a squeeze.

The paddle wheel was turning.

He attacked the warhead savagely, embracing it with both arms and running them toward the tube door in a blind search for the paddle wheel. Something slashed at his forearm with a series of light cuts. It was the wheel. Thrusting his hand into it, he succeeded in stopping it.

But now, suddenly, his air was gone. Excitement

and exertion had burned the oxygen out of his lungs. He worked the screwdriver into the aperture in which the wheel was set, trying to jam it. At last it wedged itself and he backed his hand carefully from the wheel. The pain in his lungs was like the scalding of steam. But the wheel was stopped.

He shot to the surface with a single downstroke of both arms. Several seaman were leaning overside to look for him.

"How's about it?" one of them shouted.

"It's stopped!" Keith gasped. "I'll need a chock of wood and a hammer to do it right."

The hammer was there before he had his breath. With it came a chock made from the end of a lettuce crate. He wedged the tapered end of the chock between the paddle wheel and the side of the aperture and pounded it home with slow underwater strokes. When it was firmly set, he drove the screwdriver into the other side of the aperture.

Someone dropped a line and he clung to it while they pulled him up, shivering with cold and excitement.

"Good goin'!" a crewman said, slamming him on the back.

"Good going? I'm the one that fired it!" Keith said weakly.

14

Mako tiptoed sheepishly to within three miles of San Diego's outer harbor, where she was met by a submarine rescue vessel. Underwater demolition men swam down to examine the fouled torpedo by searchlight. Divers cut away the door of Tube Six and the fish was drawn out with block and tackle. For the first time in eighteen hours, the crew relaxed.

All but Torpedoman Apprentice Stocker.

He surmised that the word must have been passed to leave him alone. Beyond Jolley's curt announcement that he was relieved of his duties, he was not told what was going to happen. Maybe it had never happened before, he thought, and Casey was having to study Regulations to see what you did with a crazy torpedoman.

Lying on his bunk, he listened to the calls and movements attending arrival in port. Watches were set and all unessential hands given liberty. But *Mako's* muscles were still flexed. She would receive her orders any moment, and would lie at the dock only until the fuel tanks were topped off, supplies taken aboard, and her mysterious executive officer ushered in.

Hector came forward after the last man had left the torpedo compartment. He sat on the bunk twisting his white cap.

"Tough luck, kid. What happened?"

"I was daydreaming. I reached for the wrong firing lever."

Hec wagged his head, suddenly whacked him on the knee and stood up. "Gotta run, Stock. Scobie's holding a ride for me. Too bad you can't come along and see the big town."

"I've seen it. Take it easy, Hec."

A few minutes later, a speaker snapped on. "Torpedoman Stocker to the wardroom."

Alone in the wardroom, Casey sat at the long table writing a letter. His thick brown hair was combed straight back and he was frowning as he wrote. He was coatless, with his sleeves rolled up. Keith rapped on the door jamb.

"Come in," Casey said.

He finished the letter and set it aside. Then with a scowl he demanded:

"What went wrong yesterday?"

"I dropped the ball, Captain. I don't know why."

Casey shook his head. "Are you having problems?"

"No, sir."

"Do you like subs?"

"Yes, sir."

"Then what went wrong?" Casey kept biting in like a drill.

Keith glanced up at the overhead, then down at his feet. "Well, there was this book I'd been reading before I went on watch."

"Comic book, no doubt?"

"A sonar training manual. I kept thinking about it and my mind wandered for a minute."

The speaker behind Casey grated. "Captain, conn. Your new exec requests permission to come aboard."

"About time! Send him down."

"Shall I come back later?" Keith asked.

"No. You might as well meet him now. You'll have a lot more grief with the exec than you will with your skipper, I can promise you. All I have to do is make the rules. He has to enforce them."

A big, sober, man with a tanned face and craggy eyebrows appeared at the door. Under his arm he carried a flat walnut box that looked like a case for artist's paints. He wore a lieutenant's boards on his crisp gabardine coat. His hands were big and knobby, and there was thick blond hair over them. He tapped with the side of his shoe against the bulkhead. "Come in," Casey said. The executive officer stepped into the wardroom and offered the skipper his mimeographed orders.

"Ratkowski, Myron R., Captain," he said in a slow, easy voice.

Casey stood up, shook hands with him, and introduced Keith, who was already standing. "Began to think I didn't rate an executive officer," Casey said. "How'd it happen you didn't join us at Mare Island?"

"I've been in the Naval Hospital down here, sir," Ratkowski said. "They just released me yesterday."

"How're you feeling?"

"Fine, Captain."

"I see you're a demon navigator," Casey said, nodding at the case under Ratkowski's arm. "Boxed sextant, eh? Top in your class?"

"That's right."

"What ship do you come from?"

Ratkowski frowned. "I was on *Rockfish*."

"Oh." For a moment the skipper seemed stopped. He twisted a ruby ring on his finger. Then: "Hell, don't stand there! Sit down! Take off your coat. *Rockfish*. I'll be damned! How many of you got off her?"

"One," said Ratkowski, Myron, U.S.N. "Three of us escaped, but the others died later."

Keith could only infer that the submarine *Rockfish* had been sunk, and that the executive officer had been the only survivor. He looked at him now in awe.

"How'd it happen?" asked Casey.

"If you don't mind, sir—"

"I do mind!" Casey said quietly. "If you can't talk about it, then you aren't ready for sea duty."

Ratkowski hung his coat over the back of a chair. He made a nervous grin at Casey and said:

"Right you are, Captain. I haven't talked about it because it's still painful. But maybe the best therapy is to verbalize it, as they say. We took a depth charge in the Solomons and sank in ninety feet of water. There were fifteen of us in the forward torpedo compartment. We tried to get out with Momsen lungs. Three of us reached the surface alive and headed for an island. Sharks got the other men. I was picked up by a PT-boat a few days later."

"What island?"

"Vella Lavella. Jap-held."

"What about the men in the after compartments? Think any of them might have made it?"

"Could have. It was at night and I didn't see anybody. We opened up at about the control room. We were rigged for depth charge, or it would have been over in ten seconds. I don't know how far aft the blast extended."

He had picked up a pencil and was rolling it between his palms while he talked slowly and matter-of-factly, as though nothing he said was of great consequence.

"How'r'ya feeling now?" Casey asked him. "Ready for duty?"

The exec nodded slowly. "I'm going to write my name on every fish on the boat so they'll know who mailed it to them."

Keith felt as though he should leave, but the fact was that a disciplinary action had been about to take place when the executive officer arrived, and things had not changed in that respect. Ratkowski cleared his throat.

"By the way, there's no gangway watch topside. You'll probably want to note it down in your Mast Book."

"I don't keep a Mast Book." Casey shrugged. The Captain's Mast Book was the formal record of all sins committed aboard a ship. It was generally conceded by officers to be at least as essential as a helm. The exec stared at the captain.

"If anybody gets out of line," Casey explained, "I have the soles stripped from his feet and cured with battery juice. If that doesn't civilize him, I have him fired out of a torpedo tube—Number Six tube, usually," he added, with a glance over at Keith.

"I see," the exec commented, obviously trying to understand how a ship could be run without discipline.

"Which brings us to the torp who fired Number Six yesterday," said Casey ominously. He explained tersely what had happened. "Of course," he conceded, "it wasn't the first mistake that's been made aboard this ship, and it probably won't be the last."

"No, sir," Ratkowski said thoughtfully. "And some of the subs that mistakes have been made on are lying in the coral now."

"We'd be on the bottom ourselves, except that Stocker dived overside and jammed the arming mechanism. That's why I feel he can't be all bad. He wants to be a sonarman," he added reflectively.

The exec raised his eyebrows. "Who stands sonar watches?" he inquired.

"A fireman and an electrician's mate."

"What makes you think you'd be a good sound man?" Ratkowski asked Keith, his brown, angular face skeptical.

"Just that I'm interested in sea sounds, and—I don't know." Keith shrugged. "I used to goggle-fish and I feel that it would come naturally. We didn't have much instruction in it at New London, but it came easy for me."

Casey turned leaves in a folder open before him and said judicially: "He's got the elements. Physically at least. Fifteen-fifteen ears, twenty-twenty vision."

"I taught at the Fleet Sonar School for six months. If you want, I'll try to knock him into some kind of shape for you."

"Do that."

Casey pointed a finger at Keith. "Whatever you

do on this boat hereafter, do it like you loved it! Whether you're standing a galley watch or greasing ammo. I don't keep a Mast Book but I've got a wicked memory, and in my game two strikes sends you to the showers. Clear?"

"Yes, sir!"

"Whether you stay on *Mako* or not depends on what Mister Ratkowski tells me about you when we reach Pearl. That won't be long."

"Yessir!" Keith gulped.

Casey dug in his pocket. "Here's a couple of bucks. Take a bus to town and get me a pair of knitting needles and a ball of yarn. Report back at 2400 sharp."

"Uh—what color?" Keith asked. He knew the skipper well enough by now to know that he was serious about his kidding.

"Any color. You're relieved."

Casey was still awake, studying charts in the wardroom, when Keith returned with some of the other men he had encountered in San Diego. Mister Ratkowski was with him, measuring distances with a pair of calipers. He was smoking a cigar and had his shirt sleeves rolled up. Keith presented the package containing the needles and yarn.

"Excuse me a minute," Casey said.

Keith watched him write on a pad of paper: "As

long as you're going to be an old woman about this ship, Chief, you might as well go the whole route." Casey stuffed the note into the package and handed it back to Keith.

"Just put it on the chief's bunk. I haven't seen a dirty deck in so long I feel like I'm on a training ship. And keep this to yourself."

15

Mako was stuffed with supplies like a turkey with dressing. Big, gleaming torpedoes slid down the loading hatches into the fore and aft torpedo compartments—warshots with torpex in their noses. Frozen food was crammed into her. Four-inch shells were carried aboard, and cases of twenty-millimeter ammunition. Fresh water and fuel oil rushed into her hard tanks. Every petty officer had an axe to grind, and they bickered like shrews when one had to wait for the other's supplies to go aboard.

"You'll have a gay time fighting this war without fuel oil!"

"Fine! You got any delicious recipes for oil, Rainey? I ain't got a big brain like yours, I'm only the cook, but if I don't get my food aboard we'll be eating creamed nuts and bolts before we reach Pearl!"

That night, with every locker straining its hinges, the submarine slipped past Point Loma and breasted the long, slow rolls of the sea. It was October and the weather was clear. Beyond the Coronado Islands a cold wind whistled through the antennae and rigging. Keith stood the starboard lookout, wearing a submarine jacket and searching the dark waters through binoculars. Yet he knew he was little better than blind during the dark hours. The real lookouts were below—the sound and radar men.

It was 2000, eight o'clock, when Toro Hartman climbed out on the bridge and yawned,

"Fresh doughnuts in the messhall. You're relieved."

Keith carried the sonar manual to one of the tables. A motor-machinist's mate in oil-soaked dungarees brought coffee to his table and sat down to sweeten a doughnut in the sugarbowl. A powerful odor of sweat and oil began to spread around him. On the new boats, the engine room and maneuvering room were the only compartments which were not air-conditioned.

"Holy Ned!" the cook exclaimed. "Get out of here, Rainey, you turn my stomach!"

Rainey, the motor mach, glanced up and then fell to eating again. "I'm just going on watch. Relax."

"Get out! That fuel-oil smell, to mention *just one*, gets into the bread dough I'm setting."

Rainey grumbled and carried his coffee and doughnuts aft to the engine room. No one, including the skipper, wanted to make an enemy of the ship's cook.

". . . On the other hand," Keith read, "the rattle of chainfalls in a torpedo room may easily be mistaken for the sound of a torpedo."

A door opened and closed. Casey and Mister Ratkowski came through on inspection. The exec gazed around at the soft-green bulkheads with faint disapproval. He was wearing red dark-adaption glasses preparatory to going on watch topside.

"What do you think about getting silhouettes up tonight?"

"Nuts to that," Casey said. "What've we got silhouette books for? No man aboard can memorize one-tenth of the ships we'll see."

As they went forward, Keith heard him ask: "Have our colors been taken in?"

"No, sir, you said you wanted them left up."

"Well, take them in now and stow them in the locker."

Keith closed his book a few moments later. He had a practice watch at the sound gear coming up at 0600 and decided to turn in. Just then the captain's voice came clearly over the loudspeaker.

"Clear the bridge! Dive, dive!"

The raucous warning of the diving alarm filled the ship. Everyone jumped up, startled. Becket, electrician's mate first class, reached for the battle phones on the wall.

"All hands up for diving stations!" he bawled, pulling on the phones.

"Is this a battle stations?" a young seaman called.

"You didn't hear the alarm, did you?" Becket snarled. A middle-aged man with pouched, jaded eyes and a yellowish face, he crouched against the wall at the end of a bench, listening to the calls and relaying them to the crew to keep them advised of what was happening. Calls that concerned the entire ship would come over the loudspeaker.

Doors and hatches were slamming and a few voices penetrated to the messroom. The cook let himself carefully down on a bench.

"Main induction shut and locked," Becket muttered.

The grinding throb of the diesels faded.

Suddenly the loudspeaker crackled. Lieutenant Bratton's voice came through. "Mister Ratkowski is still topside, Captain! Request permission to surface!"

There was a shocked quiet. Then Becket repeated the captain's answer, which he had received through the phones.

"*Negative on that! Negative!*" he repeated, looking around the room.

"Repeat?" the loudspeaker said.

"*Negative!*" Becket said huskily. Then he began phone-talking again, like a man talking in his sleep: "Two-eight feet. Three-five feet. All compartments report from forward aft."

Like a row of dominoes toppling over, the talkers in the compartments reported in.

Then the skipper's voice drawled: "All back full. Left full rudder."

The slowing of the ship was instantly felt; everyone swayed forward. "You mean," Soper whispered, "the exec is still on the bridge and the Old Man ain't lettin' him in?"

"I don't know what the blazes he's doin'," Becket growled, adjusting his phones. "Prepare to surface," he resumed.

There was a clang as the main induction, which was the ship's windpipe, opened hydraulically. A diesel roared into action. Three others added their sixteen-hundred-horsepower shouts. The pressure sighed out with the opening of the conning tower hatch.

"Mister Ratkowski aboard," Becket said.

Spoons began slowly to stir forgotten coffee. Becket hung up the phones, as arguments grew on the meaning of the brief dive-and-surface routine. Presently the skipper cleared everything up.

"That was a fairly good drill," he announced over the speaker. "There was one near-casualty, which I don't think will happen again. We're supposed to be combat-ready. Hereafter, a life belt will be attached to the periscope at all times, in case a man is left topside. Remember: you've got eleven seconds to get below, whether you're dumping garbage or recovering the colors."

Keith climbed onto his bunk in the torpedo room. A single light burned. Chief Jolley was lying on an unoccupied bunk, staring at the overhead. The compartment was beginning to resound to the snoring of weary crewmen.

"Where were you at, Stocker?" he asked.

"I was in the messroom, Chief. I'd just come off watch."

"I was in the control room, and if you ask me, that was dirty pool. The Old Man gave the alarm when he knew the X.O. was clear back on the cigarette deck. The conning tower shoulda counted them in and out, but this bunch is still greener'n ripe cheese. You ask me, he did it apurpose."

It had seemed that way to Keith, too. He kept quiet and let the chief talk it out.

"You never see anything so wet! But was he cool! He just hands his wrist watch to Rubio and says, 'Hang this in the engine room, where it'll have a chance to dry.' He didn't bat an eye."

"Maybe that's what the skipper wanted to find out," Keith said.

"What?"

"Whether he'd be cool in an emergency."

"Why wouldn't he be?"

"Well, coming off the *Rockfish*."

Jolley reared up. "The X.O. was on *Rockfish?*"

"He said so. Only known survivor."

Jolley relaxed onto the hard pad. "That's it, then! The Old Man wanted to find out this side of Pearl, so he could replace him. That's it."

Ship sounds took over: the muted coffee-grinder rumble of the diesels; a mysterious pounding; distant voices.

"Yessir! The skipper was using his head. Because there ain't many dime stores in the Yellow Sea where you can buy a new exec, if the old one should cave in."

Becket was at the sonar stack when the executive officer led Keith to the conning tower in the morning. Engrossed in a Western magazine half hidden in his lap, the portly, sad-eyed submariner in his skivvy shirt did not hear them arrive. Wearing headphones, he turned a page and then reached up to twist a small crank back and forth without interrupting his reading. The sonar console was a compact board of gauges and knobs, vertically arranged and with a small crank at a lower corner.

"Becket!" the exec boomed.

Becket turned smoothly on the swivel seat and the magazine magically disappeared. He smiled and said innocently:

"All quiet, sir."

"Switch to sonar loudspeaker," said the exec sternly.

Becket threw a switch. The pulse beats of the ocean filled the compartment with a subdued roar. Darting in and out through this dull fabric of sound were many thin, bright filaments of noise.

"Let's listen around for a minute," Ratkowski said.

He twisted the crank slowly. Almost immediately a sound of distant scraping came up. "Bearing one eight zero," he said. "Have you checked it?"

"Oh, it's just them jokers in the galley," said Becket. "Soper's cleaning a grease vent with a chain pad, I reckon."

"You *reckon?*" the lieutenant commander repeated.

"I'll check," Becket said, picking up a phone. "Galley, conn," he said. "Are you making that racket I'm pickin' up on the sound gear? Well, knock it off, how about it, hey? Mister Ratkowski's takin' a sweep."

The noise ended at once.

"It *could* have been a boat," Mister Ratkowski said.

"Yes, sir, but not likely. The rhythm wasn't steady."

Ratkowski grunted and dialed around. "Okay, you're relieved," he told Becket. The sonarman departed, and the exec told Keith to take his place. He turned down the volume on the loudspeaker.

The conning tower was quiet except for the soft frying sound from the sonar speaker and an occasional word from the junior officer of the deck to Rubio, standing a helm watch.

"God knows we need a decent sonarman on this boat," the exec said impatiently. "Did you see Becket reading that Western magazine? He was listening, of course, but the point is, he was bored. A good sonarman is never bored. When his watch is over, he's as sharp as he was at the beginning. Take another sweep around," he said.

Keith dialed completely around once more and heard no single noises.

"You said you like goggle-fishing?"

"Yes, sir."

"Ever hunt?"

"Some. My dad was quite a hunter."

"I've noticed that men with a love of nature, let's say, make the best sonarmen. To them, the ocean is like the woods. It's full of tracks and other indications of life. They're always noticing these things and trying to understand them. The best sonarman I ever trained was a farm boy. That kid *thought* like a fish! His mind was below the surface, and he used this *instinct* to decide whether he'd heard a ship with a loose crankshaft or a whale with a stomachache."

He switched off the loudspeaker. "Okay, put on

the phones. Keep dialing around, and make your reports to the JOD every half-hour."

For three days *Mako* plunged west and south, through seas which were becoming warmer. Constant drills kept the crew taut: battle stations surface, battle stations submerged, depth charge, collision in the conning tower, fire drills. Between drills there were watches to stand. Keith stood no watches other than sonar during this period, but Mister Ratkowski was likely to send for him at any hour to listen to something.

"Hear that? What is it?"

An unbroken sizzling noise vibrated the earphones. "Rain, sir."

"Why?"

"Because it sounds like rain, and the bearing is all around the compass."

"And don't you forget it! Sometime we'll be looking for a rain squall to hide in!"

And another time: "What's that?" They were at the duplicate sound gear in the forward torpedo room, while Becket had the watch in the conning tower.

The sound was a laboring weee-chug! weee-chug! A picture popped into his mind: a small freighter bucking along through a heavy sea. It had the background of a Connecticut coastline. This one he remembered.

"AK, sir. Old and not very big. The shaft sounds squeaky."

"Becket calls it a big one."

With a single screw? Keith thought.

Sometime later the lookout reported a small cargo vessel off the starboard bow. "O.K.," the exec said. "You're relieved."

But one morning it was a fast, angry, *Chow, chow, chow!* which brought the hairs up on his neck. The noise was savage and powerful. He could hear two screws beating the water, and visualized a warship bearing down on them with a bone in her teeth.

"Destroyer!" Keith said. His inclination was to get under a bunk for protection when the collision came. He could hear the heavy washing of the bow wave as the ship charged them.

"It's one of our destroyers, and she's already given us an A-A. She'll escort us into the harbor."

"Pearl?"

The executive officer nodded. Despite his sureness, the gray-green eyes seemed to flinch as he turned down the rising volume of the destroyer's screw sounds.

"One of these days soon," he muttered, "it will be a Japanese destroyer, or a couple of them, and they'll throw ashcans at us; and believe you me, Stocker, there'll be a lot less horseplay and high spirits on this boiler after that!"

He closed his mouth abruptly. He had spoken quickly and in anger.

"Very well," he said, "I'll certify you for sonar duty." He said crisply to the Chief of the Boat, "Pass the word to secure from sea detail; on deck the maneuvering watch."

At the steering gear, Becket took his eyes from the compass. "Hey, how about liberty, Mister Ratkowski?"

"Not as far as I'm concerned. We're here to pick up our orders and go out on patrol. No use breaking whatever good habits we've picked up since we left."

The exec went forward to confer with the skipper. Becket's bleary eye followed him through the oval-shaped doorway. "That guy wouldn't give you the sleeves out of his vest."

Mako entered Pearl Harbor with her colors fluttering. Still ringed with a broad black band of oil, the harbor remembered the great ships that had been ripped open by Japanese bombs less than a year ago. Here and there the rusting remains of a battleship showed above the water. Keith recalled the black clouds of that December morning, the dive bombers slashing in, the vast erupting roars from the harbor, and the terror that had swept the island like an epidemic.

But now Hawaii had caught her breath. Rivet

guns clattered instead of machine guns; steel-helmeted workmen swarmed in the Navy Yard. Above Hickman Field, anchored blimps drifted. American planes and ships shuttled in and out, veterans of Coral Sea and Midway, as well as unblooded vessels like U.S.S. *Mako*. Far to the west, other planes and ships were killing and being killed in a valiant fight to keep the Marines supplied on Guadalcanal, where what was to have been a swift and easy campaign had already blazed out of control for three months.

As the submarine passed Ten-Ten dock, the main communication circuit crackled. "Sea and anchor details lay topside! All line-handlers lay topside!" A moment later, Casey's voice announced liberty till 0700 the following morning for all but a security watch. The yeoman posted a list of men who would remain aboard, which included Keith. Noisy shipmates in liberty whites streamed through the control room for check-off. Someone shouted at Rubio, as he swung up the ladder:

"Hey, Hec! How's about ten till payday?"

"Sorry, amigo," Hec called down. "I got all my funds tied up in the Pan American Highway."

As Keith was going forward, he heard Captain Casey's voice in the skipper's cabin. "You should have told me, then, and I wouldn't have given them liberty. I didn't know you were already on record as against it."

"I just assumed you wouldn't want them going ashore," Ratkowski's voice replied. "Half of them will come back somewhat the worse for wear and hardly in shape for duty."

"They'll be back to normal in twenty-four hours and we won't be on station for days. And don't forget, each liberty a man gets in the submarine war may be his last."

"Right you are, Captain," Mister Ratkowski said. "Does that apply to executive officers too?"

"It does," chuckled Casey. "And don't let me see you back here before 0700 either."

16

Keith was in the messroom having early lunch. Scattered about were other men who had an afternoon watch coming up. At another table, Rubio was in an acey-deucey game. Chief Jolley was having a cigarette and a cup of coffee. For several days the submarine had traveled southwest, penetrating the hot equatorial currents. By night she cruised on the surface, snowy foam swishing through her black deck slats leaving a swath of phosphorescence behind her. By day she moved below the surface, hiding from enemy patrol planes.

Skivvy shirts and dungarees were the new uniform, the trousers often being cut off at the knees. Many of the crewmen had started moustaches and beards, though the heat was against anything more luxurious than a goatee. The air conditioner wrung gallons of water from the tropical air but failed to bring the temperature below a hundred degrees. In the engine room, the red line frequently stood above 120 degrees.

Mako's orders directed her to the Solomon Islands, where Japan was trying with all her sea power to isolate the American forces struggling to take Guadalcanal. For weeks destroyers, cruisers, and aircraft had clashed in savage engagements. By day the Americans on the malarial island held their own. But at night the Imperial Japanese Navy heavyweights came churning down the narrow channels through the islands to land fresh Japanese troops and supplies. As fast as the Americans took one bloody ridge, they were thrown back from another. The Navy was hurling everything into the path of the nightly "Tokyo Express" in an attempt to blockade the island, but the warships and transports kept bulling through.

This was where *Mako* was going, with a load of twenty-four torpedoes.

As he ate, Keith was reading *The Last Gasp*, the boat's mimeographed daily paper: *"How many rivets are there in the boat? Enter the Rivet-Guessing contest and win an all-expense liberty in the Imperial Hotel, in Tokyo!"* Mister Ratkowski came aft, carrying a chart and his famous boxed sextant. He took the unoccupied space at Keith's right.

"The captain's got charts all over the wardroom table and I've got a three-star fix to work out to check our position."

"At *noon?*" Chief Jolley asked him.

"The hard way," boasted the exec. "I'm using a sun sight, a moon sight, and a sight of Venus."

One of the men at Rubio's table threw down his cards. "I ain't going to play with a guy that spends twenty-four hours a day leaning against a bulkhead figuring how to beat everybody on the boat!" he complained.

"Wait'll we cross the Equator," Hec said. "Everybody's luck will automatically change."

"Yeah, from north to south."

The engine room door opened. Soper bawled: "Shut that door! It's a hundred and five in here right now!"

Pharmacist's Mate Mike Mettick came through. "Whattayou crying about, Cookie? It's a hundred and twenty-five in the maneuvering room. I just took them something to bring the temperature down."

Soper came quickly out of his stainless-steel cubbyhole, wiping his hands on his apron. "Yeah? Like what?"

From a carton Mettick handed him a brown bottle of pills. "Salt tablets!" Soper exclaimed disgustedly. "I took one once and like to heaved."

"You got to let them melt in your mouth. Otherwise they'll turn your stomach."

"I'll tell you what turns my stomach—frustrated doctors, like you."

As Mettick departed, Mister Ratkowski made a small, precise circle on the chart. "That's it."

"Where we at?" the chief asked curiously. "Anyplace I ever heard of?"

"You'd better have! We're in the Solomons."

"For sure?"

"I'm positive."

"Hey, men!" The cardplayers looked up. "You wanta see a Japanese cruiser?"

"You making ship models now, Chief?" Soper called. "They say that's a real good hobby for old sailors."

"Just look through the periscope practically any time," Jolley said. "You'll see something, I guarandarnteeya. We're in the Solomons!"

Casey had a navigational chart of the islands tacked to a bulkhead in the control room. Then he held a briefing session for the men going on watch. On the chart the Solomons formed a string of seven long, jungle-cowled islands slanting from northwest to southeast, closely spaced and with many smaller islands and jagged coral reefs mining the waters. Their names had a lilt: Bougainville, Vella Lavella, New Georgia, San Cristobal.

Like a shark cruising the coral heads, *Mako* slipped in through Indispensable Strait, at the southeastern end of the island chain.

"Torpedo Junction, that's what the Navy calls it,"

Casey said. "Japanese subs are thicker here than sea lice. Tonight we're going up Sealark Channel to the northeast end of Guadalcanal.

"The Marines landed south of there in August. They started pushing the Japs up to the north end of the island, but then the Japanese Navy got into the act. We've hardly been able to put ashore a boatload of supplies since. Their warships stand offshore all night and shell our lines, and their bombers come down the Slot all day and plow up anything the fourteen-inch guns overlooked. Our troops are dying by the hundreds while Jap marines go ashore all day and we can't lay a hand on 'em."

He ran his finger up to another point near the tip of the island. "Now, this beach is Tassafaronga. The Japs have been making their landings here in broad daylight. We'll be in that area sometime after midnight. I keep thinking what a morale booster it would be if we could torpedo a nice transport. What do you think?"

"Yes, sir!"

"And just to keep you on your toes, I'm offering an advance in rate to the first man who spots me a target."

"He can't do that," the yeoman muttered, after the formation was dismissed. "We haven't got any rates left to give out, have we, Chief?"

Jolley rubbed the long stubble on his jaw. "I wouldn't say he *can't*. The *Navy* would probably say he can't. But he seems to be one of them C.O.'s with a talent for gettin' things he ain't supposed to have."

There were two alarms that afternoon while the submarine threaded Indispensable Strait and turned west into Sealark Channel. Low-flying bombers, showing the red "meatball" insignia of the Japanese air force, drove her deep to evade detection. When the alarms were over, *Mako* came back to periscope depth. Her luck held: sonar detected no lurking submarines.

As soon as it was dark, the order was passed that they were to surface. Control room and conning tower were redded out—illuminated by red bulbs —to accustom the bridge watch to the darkness. For a half-hour the captain had been wearing dark-adaption glasses in the wardroom as he and the navigator studied the charts. When he removed them, the darkness would seem much lighter than had he come directly from a brightly lighted compartment. Jolley ticked off Keith, Rubio, and two others as battle lookouts. They donned the red night-visibility glasses in preparation for the watch.

In the tower Casey walked the periscope around, taking a final look before he ordered the ship to the surface. He snapped the handles up and signaled: "Down 'scope."

The surfacing alarm sounded. The boat began to rise.

Hartman, the quartermaster, raised the hatch and a fall of cold water drenched him. Air roared out the opening, almost lifting him through. Sliding on the black, slippery deck, Keith and the others scrambled to the lookouts' perches. Water sprinkled down from the radar antenna. The bridge filled with officers. Aloft, the air was nearly as hot as it had been below. Eastward he saw a moonlit horizon brightened by surges of distant lightning. To the north he made out a long, high mass of land with streaks of phosphorescence showing where waves were breaking over reefs.

"Island on the starboard beam," he sang out. "Breakers at two thousand yards."

"Very well."

"Permission to start the turboblow," a voice said.

"Permission granted."

"Permission to charge batteries."

"Granted. How's our course?" Casey asked the executive officer.

Ratkowski was scrutinizing something through the target-bearing transmitter glasses. "Recommend course of three zero five."

"Come to three zero five."

The ship put her head in the water and threw off phosphorescent foam like a dog shaking itself. The quiet hum of the revolving radar mast was suddenly drowned by the burbling roar of the diesel exhausts.

An hour later, Rubio sang out: "Gunflashes at two two zero!"

"I have it," Casey said. "That's artillery fire on the island."

"Naval guns at two six zero!"

Ratkowski swung the TBT glass. "Lunga Point, Captain. Looks like three or four warships shelling the airfield."

"We could probably get within torpedo range," Casey speculated, "but they'll be there all night, anyway. Let's look for transports first."

Keith shivered with excitement and fear—fear of being wounded, of dying, of being trapped in a sunken submarine; and the greatest fear of all, that he was not man enough for his job.

The wind shifted, coming directly off Guadalcanal. A sudden, unbelievable odor made him gag.

"Would you *smell* that!" someone gasped.

"Gangrene and honeysuckle," said the executive officer. "The breath of the Islands. Rotting sailors, Marines, and Japs—the water's full of them. Human garbage."

The odor settled on the tongue like grease. Keith held his handkerchief to his nose as he scanned the horizon, trying not to vomit. After a few minutes the skipper said,

"Have reliefs sent up for the lookouts. Stocker, get yourself some coffee when your relief comes and then take over at the sound gear."

"Aye, aye, sir." He was glad to hurry below when his relief arrived.

In the messroom, the second dogwatch was gulping late supper before going on watch. Keith sat down with his coffee and a piece of pie. When he went to the conning tower to relieve Becket, the sonarman told him:

"Be on your toes, genius. The fish sound like they're draggin' chains. Fifteen-minute reports to the JOD."

They had reached the area known as Ironbottom Sound, a wide channel between Guadalcanal and little Savo Island. Here, in fiery melees, scores of large and small craft had plunged to the bottom. Supply ships making for the beachheads passed around Savo as though it were a buoy. Enemy warships hurled themselves upon these transports and freighters, and bombers and fighter planes tangled in the air and destroyed one another. Thousands of bodies floated in the shark-filled waters.

From all points of the compass came ghostly scratchings and whisperings. He thought of the ships lying deep in the coral, and wondered whether water currents could stir loose rigging and shattered gun turrets to produce such sounds.

Lights were reported on Tassafaronga Beach.

"Either they've made landings," Casey speculated, "or they're planning to."

On *Mako* no one slept. All torpedo tubes were opened and crews were at their stations. Lieutenant Ramage was conferring with Chief Jolley in the forward torpedo room. A vague squeak in the phones brought Keith's head up. He twisted the sound crank back and forth over the five miles of water between Savo Island and the Japanese-held beaches. The sound was repeated.

"Sonar contact!"

Casey's voice came through the speaker from the bridge. *"Where? Whereaway?"*

"Bearing two eight zero! A ship is pinging."

An officer turned on the sonar loudspeaker. The redded-out compartment resounded to the rasping emptiness of the ocean and the regular *pings* which punctuated it. Ratkowski dropped through the hatch and listened for a moment.

"He's echo ranging all right. But he's bound to be getting back so many echoes from wrecks that he can't tell a live one from a dead one. And he can't hear our screws as far as we can hear him pinging."

"Fire-control party to the conn!" Casey ordered.

17

Ramage came panting up the ladder and got in position at the TDC, the computer which automatically set the proper course for the torpedoes once information had been fed into it. Carrying a cup of coffee, the yeoman climbed into the compartment without spilling a drop. Eight men were now crammed into the atticlike room. Casey returned to the bridge for final observations. *Mako* slowed to five knots. Speed was unnecessary, because the target was coming to her. She could pick the spot where she wanted her torpedoes and the target to meet.

The pinging became louder. Then there was a rhythmic throbbing from the sound gear—the sound of the ship's propellers. "Count the screw beats," Ratkowski ordered. He had the Is-Was hung about his neck by its cord, a slide rulelike device for quick estimation of the proper course in tracking a target. Keith passed him the count on the screw beats.

"Make it twelve knots," the exec said.

"Battle stations torpedo," Casey ordered suddenly. The alarm began bonging musically through the boat.

"Give me a range! Give me a range!" Ramage pleaded. "You can't fire without a range."

"What do you want us to do?" Ratkowski snapped. "Ping on him so he'll know we're here?"

Safety and negative tanks were already flooded so that the sub could submerge quickly when the command came. The diving officer stood by.

"Okay, we've got him!" Casey shouted down the hatch. "Range, four thousand yards. Course, one three five."

The TDC whirred as Ramage fed the data into it. *Mako* took the long sea rolls ponderously, idling toward the target course. The target was not zigging, which made tracking easy.

"Yeo!" the captain said. "Look this up: four masts, two stacks amidships, deck line high. Maybe a transport. Heavy armament fore and aft."

The yeoman pulled books from a cabinet and went through them. "Could be a *Teiko*-class transport, except for the armament."

"Probably been added," the exec rapped. "Draft?"

"Twenty-five feet, loaded."

"Set depth ten feet," the captain ordered. "Range, three five double oh. . . ."

"Fast screws at two nine zero!" Keith interrupted.

"Sounds like a destroyer. Wait, another at three zero zero!"

Ratkowski jumped to the periscope. "Up 'scope!" The seaman holding the "pickle" squeezed the switch and the periscope hummed up. The exec rode the handles, sweeping the sea in the direction Keith had indicated. Just then Casey's voice came excitedly over the speaker.

"There they are! Damn! Two DD's escorting him. We'll give him a spread at fifteen hundred. With all the noise when they explode, they may not be able to pick us up."

"What if they don't explode?"

"It's the only shot we're going to have, Mister Ratkowski. If we don't make it stick, that transport will be unloading tonight. Clear the bridge! Take her to six-five feet."

The officers who had been on the bridge with him descended to the conning tower. Ratkowski crouched by the hatch to relay the captain's orders. The hatch was closed and dogged. The noise of the diesels faded, and as their vibration died reception became better in the sound gear. Keith felt sweat running down his chest. The powerful *chow-chow-chow!* of the destroyers mounted until he could visualize the ships bearing down on them. Yet they were still two miles away. Casey crouched at the periscope.

"Range—mark!"

"Two nine double oh!"

"All ahead full."

The propellers took a stronger bite at the waters of Ironbottom Sound. Keith was getting all kinds of noises in the phones—fish sounds, mysterious clankings, the pinging of the transport.

"Make ready the forward tubes. Match gyros forward."

The men at the diving planes stood motionless; the helmsman tensely made small adjustments with the big chrome steering wheel. Jolley would be on his toes in the torpedo room, ready to launch the fish manually if the electrical mechanism failed.

"Bearing—mark! Range—mark!"

"On the firing bearing, Captain," someone said sharply.

Casey's shout was like a battle cry. "Fire *One!* Fire *Two!* Fire *Three!*"

Mako lurched as the first torpedo was fired. There was a rumble and hiss of high-pressure air up forward. The firing key operator held the key down until the report came, "Number One tube fired electrically." He released the key and turned the selector switch to "Off," then turned the switch under Number Two to "On." As each torpedo was fired, he readied the next tube. In the finest synchronization, Lieutenant Ramage turned a crank set low in the face of the director before him, scrutinizing a stopwatch as he did so. Each torpedo was thus given a slightly different course, so that the full length of the target was covered and the chance of a hit was made greater.

Now there was a full minute to wait, in which the torpedoes made their run. Less than half a minute had passed when the destroyers' screws picked up speed. At the same time there was a slight change in bearing.

"High-speed screws on new bearings, sir! Screws have speeded up."

"They've got us on sound," Mister Ratkowski rapped. "Keep bearings coming."

"Seventy-five seconds, Captain," someone said. "Sounds like a miss."

"It can't be a miss!" Casey raged. "At this range? Sound, have you got anything?"

Just then Keith heard a solid *thump!* in the phones. "A dud!" Then, seconds later, he heard a second thump. The third was a clean miss.

"Give me a new setup!" the captain shouted. His whole manner had a new quality, a raging, furious stance like that of an old-time pug coming to the scratch with bloody face and clenched fists; the fighting determination of a man who could not be stopped.

"Can't do it on this course, Captain!" his exec reported. "Range is too short."

There was a deafening explosion in the phones.

Keith tore them off and clapped his hands over his ears in agony. The conning tower itself was shaken. "A hit!" someone yelled.

"Hit, nothing!" Casey shouted. "That was a shell. One of the tin cans is firing at our periscope! Two hundred feet! Rig for depth charge. Rig for silent running."

Mako's churning propellers drove her deep. The roar of the Japanese warship rose to an unbearable pitch. All watertight doors and bulkhead flappers were closed. The air conditioning was secured, fans and blowers turned off; all unnecessary gear was silenced. The sounds of echo ranging were becoming one continuous *peep-peep-peep* in the speaker.

"Coming on the range, now!"

As the first destroyer passed overhead, Keith put one of the phones to his ear and listened to the hysterical squeal of its echo ranging. Then he heard a splash.

"Pull in your necks!" he yelled.

Everybody grabbed hold of something. The tension rose until Keith wanted to scream. Even the veterans of three or four war patrols waited nervously for what submariners tried to describe, but always gave up with, *"You can't tell anybody else what it's like."* Keith pictured the cylindrical cans swerving down through the black water with crystal streams of bubbles trailing upward. He counted the seconds: fifteen, sixteen, seventeen. . . . *"Here it comes!"*

The explosion broke right on top of the conning tower, a solid shock wave that buckled the plating of the sub and extinguished all her lights. The conning tower went pitch-dark. Keith was knocked off his feet. Other men were sprawling on the deck, and metal objects flew like bullets. The second charge exploded close aboard. The third, fourth, and fifth hammered home like pile drivers.

"All right, let's have the emergency lights!" Casey shouted.

The emergency lights flooded the compartment. The deck was littered with chunks of cork insulation torn from the walls. Broken light globes, cigarette receptacles, and tools lay everywhere. Dust and paint chips filled the air. Although the barrage had ceased, the ship still roared with the vibrations of hundreds of pipes and fittings.

"All compartments report!"

Keith scrambled up. Mister Ratkowski was crouched before a bucket, being sick. Men were stripping off shirts and pants and draping rags about their necks to sop up the perspiration. The thermometer showed a hundred and twelve. The freight-train racket of the second warship suddenly broke through the hull.

"How much water have we got, Mister Ratkowski?" Casey asked.

"All we need."

"Take her to three hundred feet!"

The destroyer arrived with a thunderous thrashing of screws. The depth charges began to rain down. There was an audible *click* beyond the hull, then a tremendous BANG!, and a moment later a swishing of bubbles through the superstructure. As subsequent explosions slammed at the submarine, her hull whipped and twisted in torture. Deckplates and gratings clattered about like iron platters. The crew crouched with bent knees, standing clear of the bulkheads, their lips parted and their eyes staring.

The barrage ended, but now the first destroyer was roaring back. The ships were cutting figure eight's above *Mako,* dropping their ashcans at the crossover. *Why don't we get out of here? Why don't we run?* Keith wondered in panic. *Oh, God, get us away!*

WHAM!

The first destroyer was dumping her explosives on them again. The submarine writhed. The blows came from above and below. A handle popped from a valve and rolled on the deck.

The telephone talker sang out, "After battery flooding, Captain!"

"How bad?"

"Casualty undetermined."

"Isolate the flooding and abandon the compartment."

The thrumming of pipes and tubing was continuous as the barrage worked from aft forward, twisting and wrenching the submarine about. When the last explosion faded, Casey let out a roar of anger.

"Damn them! There's no sense in waiting here to be killed! Sound, pick up the other destroyer."

"Two three zero," Keith reported. "Two three five. Two four zero. He's turning."

"Make ready the forward tubes! Come to six-five feet! All ahead standard."

Ratkowski wiped his face with a towel and stared at Lieutenant Ramage. *Is he crazy?* they asked each other silently. What Casey seemed about to attempt was a bows-on attack—the down-the-throat shot, the most hazardous one in the book. It involved charging head-on at the other ship, getting off your torpedoes before he found you with his guns, and diving at the last moment to avoid a collision. It meant a target forty feet wide instead of four hundred feet. The advantages were that the range was short, and if the other skipper swerved to one side or the other, he was almost certain to take a torpedo broadside.

There was a mighty hissing and rumbling as *Mako* climbed steeply for the surface. Casey gave a shout.

"There he is! He's started back."

The TDC dials whirred: 1,600 yards, 1,500, 1,350. At 1,100 the captain ordered: "Final firing bearing and shoot."

"Fire *Four!*" *Mako* recoiled. "Fire *Five! Fire Six!*"
The fish whined away and were lost in the thrashing
of the destroyer's screws.

"They're running true," Casey reported, his brow
jammed against the eyepiece. "He hasn't seen them.
. . . Now he's firing at them!" he groaned.

The underwater explosions could be heard without sound gear. Closer explosions warned that the
destroyer was also zeroing in on the submarine's
periscope. The seconds passed.

"Number One's wide to port. Number Two's wide.
Number Three . . ." his voice drew the word out as
he watched, ". . . wide to starboard."

"Take her down?" Ratkowski asked quickly.

Casey turned the 'scope a little. "Wait, he's turning! *He's flinched! It's a hit, a blankety-blank hit!*"

A concussion wave shook the submarine. Someone
cut in the loudspeaker. The roaring of water through
a jagged rip in the destroyer's hull sounded as
though *Mako* herself had been torpedoed. There
were terrifying noises as the bulkheads crumpled.
The screws went silent. A chain of lesser explosions
followed. In the conning tower, crewmen pounded
each other on the back.

"Right in the middle!" Casey yelled. "He's coming apart like a rotten log. Control, take her down to
a hundred and fifty feet. We're going under her."

18

Mako penetrated a solid barrier of shock waves as she passed beneath the sinking destroyer. A series of explosions astern told them that the other destroyer was wildly dropping charges among the survivors. As the sound of the transport's propellers became audible, Casey went to work with the grim coolness of an executioner.

"Make ready the stern tubes. Set depth ten feet."

The transport was bending on full steam for Tassafaronga Beach. *Mako* surfaced for greater speed. Becket took Keith's place, and Keith went topside with the battle lookouts. The night was beautiful. Enormous clouds were piled high in the south; the moon glistened on the sea in long, glassy rolls. The transport had only a two-mile lead, and *Mako* was gulping it down greedily. On the bridge, the fire-control party plotted and tracked. The forward torpedo team was working against time to reload.

"We're getting in shallow water," Ratkowski warned.

"I know that," Casey snapped.

"We've only got four fish left, and we can't count on the after battery if we have to go deep."

Casey said: "I'm going to sink that transport, Mister Ratkowski. Those Jap marines aren't going ashore any way but dead."

The transport was running straight, desperately trying to make the landing beach. Bearings were automatically flashed from the TBT on the bridge to the torpedo officer. Casey took a final look-see as the *maru* came on the firing bearing.

"*Fire!*"

The fish ran out, a luminous wake spreading behind it as broad as a highway.

"*Fire!*"

"*Fire!*"

"*Fire!*"

A blue-white flash tore the night apart, mounting a thousand feet into the sky. In the core of the flash could be seen the transport, its stern ripped away. Then another fish slashed open his belly and a dazzling display of fireworks erupted. "Ammunition locker!" Casey chortled. "*Ain't* that beautiful!"

Multicolored rockets and star shells illuminated the sea like a Fourth of July celebration. A series of crumpling explosions shredded the transport. In sixty seconds nothing was left but scraps of flotsam burning like paper.

Casey gave all hands in the conn a look through

the periscope. When his turn came, Keith took a quick glance and then closed his eyes and only pretended to look. All he could think of was men being burned black and dumped in the water; the rapacious sharks of Ironbottom Sound, and the hundreds of crewmen who would be trapped below-decks and cooked in live steam. It was too much like the ending of the *Bataan Trader*.

It had to be done. But he didn't want to see it.

"Maybe we ought to swing by and make sure that there aren't any survivors," the captain speculated.

"There couldn't be many," Mister Bratton said uneasily.

"Any is too many. I'd like an old-fashioned machine gun shoot, myself. Any of those lice that get ashore will be in the lines as soon as they dry 'em off."

They thought he was joking, but he was serious. It took every officer on the bridge to talk him out of it. The other destroyer would be here in minutes. He hated those soldiers as much in the water as he had hated them on the ship. They were still the enemy, though dying. Keith was reminded of hunting with his father; the way he had always weakened at the moment when he had the quail or rabbit in the open and then he needed only to pull the trigger.

His father used to tell him, "If you're going to

hunt, hunt. Don't bring a gun along to study nature."

Captain Casey, too, was a natural-born hunter.

Running deep and silent, *Mako* crept around Cape Esperance and into the open sea south of Guadalcanal. She had wounds to lick and tubes to reload. She had been bloodied in battle, and now she drove her prow through the swells so that she seemed almost alive. On her first combat patrol, she had sunk a warship and a transport.

In the crew's mess, all conversation was about *Mako*. "Did you feel her pick up when she smelled that bucket? She knew she had him!"

"Yeah, and did you notice something else? Every one of them stern fish ran hot!"

"Man, did she soak up the punishment! But all it did was make her sore."

Chief Jolley came in and looked over the messroom. He was stripped to the waist, and the deep, hairy barrel of his chest was matted with sweat.

"What's to eat, Cookie? You been sitting on your duff all this time?"

"I been doin' my work, Chief, how about you? What went wrong with all your fish tonight?"

Jolley sat near Keith with a piece of pie. As Keith was leaving, the chief growled:

"You were right about that lousy Mark XIV torpedo. No wonder it's classified. They're ashamed to talk about it!"

19

Mako idled the next day before starting up "The Slot," the wide alley through the Solomons down which Japanese planes and ships roared in their supply and bombardment runs on Guadalcanal. A number of the submarine's sea valves had been unseated by the depth charging, and this had resulted in leakage. With these repaired, light bulbs replaced, and ten fresh torpedoes gleaming in her tube nests, she was ready for action.

Less than three hundred miles long, The Slot could be traversed by a sub in a day and a night. She might pass without seeing a single ship; or she might run into a fleet of twenty Japanese warships coming down to investigate reports of American naval activity off Santa Isabel Island. Planes reconnoitered the islands continually. Casey's dream was of surprising a fat convoy and sinking every ship in it.

"You can have the cruisers and destroyers. All I want is the tankers and transports. Is that asking too much?"

"No, sir," said Toro Hartman, as he finished a quart of reconstituted powdered milk. Casey had stopped in the crew's mess on the way through the ship, on one of his rare and reluctant inspections. He was sitting across from the big quartermaster, who was consuming an after-watch snack. Keith and a few other men were loafing in the compartment and at one table Rubio was modestly winning everything in a poker game.

"A whole convoy—a clean sweep!" Casey exclaimed. "Of course, it's probably too late on this patrol, we've only got fourteen fish left. What do you think, Hartman?"

"Never give up the ship," Toro counseled, his mouth full.

Casey grinned. "I'll tell you another thing we're going to do before this war's over: sneak right into Tokyo Bay and sink a battleship!"

"I hope he's kidding!" muttered Keith.

"He's never kidding," Pharmacist's Mate Mettick sighed.

Casey finished his coffee and stood up. "Oh, by the way. I'm organizing a Boy Scout troop. Any volunteers?"

"Has it got anything to do with scraping paint?" Rubio asked.

"No, but it's got a lot to do with throwing hand grenades. Once in a while we're going to sight a ship that isn't worth wasting a torpedo on, or else it's too shallow. In that case, we'll use the deck guns, and if there's any resistance we'll have to resort to things like hand grenades."

"Any extra pay?" Hartman asked.

"Just a medal if you're killed. I'd like you to head it for me. How about it?"

Hartman shrugged. "Okay."

"Anybody else? Soper, how about you?"

"You'll be sorry, Captain," Soper growled, "if I'm killed and you have to cook your own chow. Okay, I'm in."

They reached Choiseul Island, one of the northerly islands in the chain. Choiseul was a long, low, beautiful island cloaked in jungle vines and trees. From a distance you could not smell the rotting vegetation. You could not see the black leeches that infested the rivers, nor the mosquitoes that carried several different kinds of malaria. What you could see were coral beaches and green shallows deepening rapidly into darker greens and then blue-black. With binoculars you could sometimes discern a smear of smoke—like the smoke the officer who had the periscope watch saw at 1450.

"Captain to the conn! Smoke at three four zero!"

There was the usual confusion in the ship, then the tense feeling of readiness. The approach party bent over the charts, the fire-control party jammed the conning tower. In a few minutes the source of

121

the smoke was identified: a "Sugar Charlie" was sneaking down the coast close to shore. A Sugar Charlie was a small sea truck used for interisland transport. It had a single cargo well amidships, with a high bow and stern. On the assumption that it had no detection equipment, they closed to within two thousands yards and studied it.

"I'm not going to waste a torpedo on a thing like that," the skipper growled.

"You going to let him go, sir?" Hartman asked.

"No, we'll sink him with the deck gun."

The gun crew was alerted and weapons for Hartman's Boy Scout troop were broken out of stowage. *Mako* carried a four-inch gun, which would blow quite a hole in a small ship. The Sugar Charlie smoked along, the low green mountains behind him topped with a moist cloud cover.

"We'll give them a chance to get into lifeboats," Casey decided. "Stand by for a battle surface. All men on gun crews get ready. Helmsman, steady as you go."

"He's got a field gun lashed to the deck!" Ratkowski reported suddenly.

"Nuts. He probably doesn't even know how to fire it." The alarm sounded for a battle stations surface. *Mako* surfaced with a roar of cascading water. Scobie, the chunky little gunner's mate, led his gun crew out with plugs of cotton tucked into their ears.

Keith scrambled to his perch with the other battle

lookouts. He had a forward position so that he could see what went on. Through the glasses he watched black-haired crewmen in ragged shorts staring at the whalelike apparition which had surfaced so close to their ship. Barefoot, they ran frantically over the deck; one man ducked into the cabin. Bells jingled frantically.

Casey gave the signal to fire a ranging shot.

From the deck gun, a dazzling flash of yellow-white flame burst out over the water. A cloud of acrid white smoke with brown edges and streaks of pale blue trailed it. The shock wave that followed made Keith's ears ring. Three of the freighter's deck-hands rushed to man the field gun.

"Okay, they asked for it," Casey said. "Fire for effect."

Heat and concussion shook the gun crew. On the Sugar Charlie's deck, gun and crew disintegrated. White wood splinters filled the air. Casey stared.

"Good Lord! That gun was a dummy! The little so-and-so's were bluffing!"

At one-third speed, the sub moved in to a hundred feet. A *pup-pup-pup* of machine gun fire blazed from a porthole of the freighter. Bullets began to rattle off the bridge coaming; the officers ducked. Hartman, kneeling on the afterdeck, cut loose with a tommy gun as the machine gun crew on the cigarette deck went into action. The wood around the porthole splintered, then disintegrated. Scobie's gun crew worked fast, blasting four-inch shells into the wooden hull as fast as they could reload. The Sugar Charlie began to list. The bullnose of the sub jarred heavily against the boat.

Keith heard a throbbing sound and thought it was a pump starting up. Then he realized it was his heart. He tried to watch the action, but when he saw the wounded he had to look away. Screams and gunshots carried across the water. Then there was no more gunfire and the water was reddening with blood as the freighter began to sink.

"Let's have a few grenades for practice," Casey shouted down to Hartman's bunch. "Can you make it?"

Most of the grenades fell short and exploded underwater. Some landed on the tilting deck and a few dropped in the open hold. A minute later, there was nothing on the surface of the water but oil, smoking wood, and wounded survivors.

"Throw them some life jackets," the skipper said. "Then let's get the devil out of here."

Soper dished up strawberry shortcake that night. The berries oozed a scarlet nectar, and had been mashed into a delicious pulp. For some reason, however, many men did not eat the shortcake. Hurt and puzzled, Soper handed Mister Ratkowski a second portion when he came through the messhall.

"I ask you, sir, is there anything wrong with that shortcake?"

The exec tasted it. "It's good. It's very good."

"Then why didn't them swabbies eat it?"

"Were you on deck this afternoon?"

"Why, sure. I'm in the Boy Scout troop. Say, did you see the way Scobie blasted that so-called field piece of theirs?"

"I certainly did. And did you see the stuff hanging in the rigging afterward?"

"No. What was that?"

Soper realized suddenly what the exec was talking about. He gave up trying to sell the shortcake and threw the rest away.

Just like rabbits! Keith was thinking, as he lay in the dim torpedo room. *Just like rabbits.* But the captain was right: they had asked for it. *Somebody's got to do it. They're the killers. We're just the hangmen. Somebody's got to do it.*

20

Two days passed. *Mako,* growing restless, prowled the Solomons irritably. Frequently smoke was sighted on the horizon, but the ships' courses took them out of range. By day increased air activity forced her to hold to the deep water where a bomber could not trap her in the shallows.

Casey requested and received by radio permission to work north toward the Palau Group and try for some of the shipping in Malakal Passage. Millions of tons of war matériel were going through this passage to the Japanese naval and air bases on that island group, but American subs so far had had little luck in finding targets.

Casey had Ratkowski figure a course, and they headed northwest. At 0900, the radioman hurried from the radio room. In his cabin Casey was running an electric shaver over his jaws.

"Excuse me, Captain! I just picked this up!"

The captain read the scrawled message, " 'Radio Noumea from IJN aircraft. This message will not be repeated. We have sighted a derelict craft with Allied noncombatants. Position Latitude 630 S Longitude 15345 E.' "

"Pretty crazy, huh?" the radioman said.

"This is the whole thing?"

"Yessir. A Japanese plane reports an Allied life raft!"

"Mister Ratkowski!" Casey shouted across the companionway to the wardroom. Ratkowski came to the doorway. "Pinpoint this for me, on the double!"

When the executive officer arrived with a chart on which he had indicated the position, Casey was writing a radio message. "It's only a few hours from where we are right now, almost due west of Bougainville," the exec said.

Casey looked at the chart.

"So this so-called plane has sighted a so-called life raft. And it's radioed Admiral Halsey that if he feels like it, he can send somebody to pick up the survivors. We're probably the closest ship to it, unless they send a seaplane. What do you think we ought to do about it?"

"Nothing! Good Lord, Captain, it's a trap! What else can it be?"

"But who's going to put his foot in the trap? That's the point."

"Not us, I hope."

"Nossir. Them!" The exec and the radioman stared

at him. The skipper grinned: "If it is a trap, there's going to be a Jap sub hanging around that area waiting for a rescue party to show up. Now, if the rescuers *assume* it's a trap, then they become the trappers. Right?"

"That sub would be hard to detect, sir—"

"I detected one once before. Mostly luck, I agree. But with our new SJ radar we won't have to guess where he is, we'll know."

"Not if he's at periscope depth."

"Then we'll have to figure a way to bring him up."

Since the sky was overcast, danger from aircraft was slight. Casey surfaced and bent on full speed. He wanted the batteries at full strength and the airflasks charged. With her battle lookouts on watch, *Mako* plowed massively through the sea, her bow rising and lowering gently, a stream of troubled white water flowing aft. To stay sharp, radarmen and sonarmen stood two-hour watches. The skipper's manner was that of a man going to a big football game, excited and full of anticipation. The crew was nervous. The odds were bad enough when you were doing the stalking; but an operation like this was putting your head in the lion's mouth.

Rain squalls now obscured much of the area into which they were heading, so that radar efficiency was reduced. Sound picked up no pinging or screw sounds. Reaching the fringe of the danger area, Casey said:

"Let's take her under."

He left the radar antenna exposed. The hum of the revolving mast was audible in the conning tower. The green and amber cathode ray tubes glowed, but nothing broke the normal appearance of the screen. Keith relieved Becket at the sound gear. They pushed deeper into the trap, but still had no evidence of its teeth. At the periscope, Ratkowski bit his lip; it was clear that he did not approve of thrusting sticks into beehives. If an enemy sub were in the area, it would be lying silently at periscope depth, listening and watching. It was hard to see how Casey hoped to beat such odds. A sudden rain squall sizzled in the phones.

"There goes our visibility," the exec said, at the periscope.

"Start pinging," Casey said abruptly.

Keith looked around. "Sir?"

"Ping!" the skipper repeated. "Don't overdo it. Just make it sound like somebody was groping around."

"My God," the exec exploded, "why don't you just set off a bomb in the control room?"

Casey laughed. "What's the matter, don't you ever gamble?"

"Not when I'm holding cards like these! They can hear us echo ranging twice as far as we could get an echo!"

"Listen, Mister, the whole thing's a gamble. This is a submarine, not a yacht. The fact that they'll sell us insurance doesn't mean we're a good risk."

"But why take cards *against* yourself?"

"I'm not. I'm taking a calculated risk. We were sent out here to sink ships. Look on *Mako* as an inhabited torpedo. Sooner or later she'll probably explode, but in the meantime her sole function is to sink ships. To do that, she's got to have a little help from us."

"It doesn't seem to me we're giving her much help, sir—" Ratkowski began.

"Belay that!" Casey snapped. "I'm not running a training ship, I'm commanding a submarine; I said *ping,* and that's an order!"

Keith pressed the key and the little bullet of sound went out. The exec clamped his jaws and was silent. Casey snapped on the loudspeaker and listened to the pings going out and not coming back. *Mako* idled along at one-third speed, water whispering through her superstructure.

"Secure the echo ranging," Casey ordered. "Control, go to one hundred feet."

Keith was tense as a spring, listening for the sound of whirring screws which would mean a torpedo, since the echo ranging could bring a salvo fired on sound bearings. Casey leaned against a bulkhead, unbuttoning his shirt as the heat rose.

"Come to three five five. All ahead flank."

A moment later, Keith shouted: "Fast screws at two eight zero!"

"Pull the plug! All ahead emergency!"

Mako took a sharp angle down. The screws rose to a steady shrillness, passed overhead, and were gone. It could only have been a torpedo. A second and third passed astern. The sub strained on at emergency speed, her propellers thrashing.

Keith began to comprehend the captain's strategy, which had nearly backfired. Beyond passive sonar range, the enemy submarine had fired on sound bearings, aiming at the source of *Mako*'s echo ranging. Casey was later than he had planned in changing position. But they were still out of listening range, and soon the I-boat would know less about their presence than they knew about his.

"Come to zero zero zero," the skipper said. "Come to six-five feet. Rig for silent running."

He pressed his brow to the eyepiece as the periscope broke from the water in a sparkling cascade of droplets. They waited.

The submarine hung suspended in the water like a metal sarcophagus. There was no sound anywhere aboard; the air was dead. Heat and humidity beaded her metal skin. Keith listened around. Casey relinquished the periscope to Ratkowski, who peered through it.

"Steaming like a bathtub out there," he muttered.

Fish sounds scraped and boomed. Keith watched his dials and kept sweeping around. Something caught his attention. A soft, steady pulsation was coming from their port bow, gently disentangling itself from the other noises. The bearing needle came to rest.

"Screws at two eight five!"

Walking the periscope around, Casey peered into the hot sunshine. "Too much haze," he muttered. "Keep the bearings coming."

As the enemy bore in from their left, it grew evident that he would be too far ahead for them to fire on optical bearings. He would cross over and fade into silence without their seeing him. Casey hated to try a blind shot on sound alone, as the Japanese sub had done and failed.

"What's his speed?"

"About five knots."

"All ahead one-third."

Mako glided forward. Eventually she would be heard. The trick would be to get into firing position first.

Suddenly Casey caught his breath. "There he is! About two thousand yards! Final bearing and shoot! Bearing—mark!"

"Two nine zero."

"Set."

"Fire One!"

The expulsion of the torpedo jolted *Mako*'s shell. They fired a spread of three. Keith loosened the phones, anticipating the blast. They waited. Nothing. Casey cursed softly, his hands clenched on the periscope handles. The seconds wore away. A faint thud jarred the diaphragms of the sound gear.

"A dud!" Keith exclaimed.

"Give me a new setup!" Casey shouted.

The screws increased speed and the pitch changed as the sub began to turn away. The plotting party worked frantically as Keith called out the bearings. Dials spun softly in the torpedo data computer. But before firing keys could be pressed, the I-boat zigged away. Running deep, he twisted like an eel, seeking the black, heavy water where even a ping would not find him. In desperation, Casey fired two blind shots on a hasty plot. No response.

"I've lost him," Keith reported.

Mako had to go on the defensive. The I-boat had secured all noise-producing gear and was listening.

"Let's get out of here," Casey said wearily. "Resume base course."

He went into his cabin and poured the bitterness of seventy-six crewmen and a frustrated skipper into a message to ComSubPac. He wanted to know what it accomplished for them to risk their lives in enemy waters to fire dud torpedoes at an antagonist firing real shells and live fish. He wanted to know why Bureau of Ordnance considered the exploder in the Mark XIV torpedo so hot that even a sub skipper wasn't allowed to open it up.

"Will try to bring home a Jap torpedo for BuOrd to copy," he concluded. "Undoubtedly the best in the Pacific."

The crew was despondent. Aware that it took only one bad break to send them to the bottom, they were up against the sad truth that the things they did right would not necessarily help them. And even more, there was an odd feeling of letting *Mako* down. It was impossible not to regard her as somehow a live creature. A spirited one, and one with a spirit that could be broken.

"A little more of this bilge," Chief Jolley said, "and she's going to get discouraged. I was on a discouraged boat, once. I don't ever want to be on another."

21

A few hours later, the skipper gave the order to change course. There was no sense in paddling all the way up to the Palaus with nine defective torpedoes aboard.

"Do they send infantrymen out with blank cartridges? Do they send the fly-boys out with training bombs? No! And they aren't sending *us* out again with a load of fish like these."

"I don't know what you can do about it," Ratkowski said, shrugging. Keith, standing a lookout watch, listened to them down on the bridge. "It seems to be the way we have to fight the war. We had fifteen duds on the *Rockfish* one time."

"And look what happened to *Rockfish*. I've had my share of duds, too, but there were always enough Mark X's aboard to insure a few kills. Now they're giving all the Mark X's to the old Sugar boats, and we get these Chinese copies of a Bangalore torpedo."

"What are you going to do, ask for Japanese torpedoes?"

"I'm going to tow one home, if I get a chance. Bureau of Ordnance might learn something. But for the present—" Casey turned to the waterproof bridge speaker, "Chief of the Boat to the bridge, on the double!"

It could not have been over ten seconds before Jolley's voice called through the hatch: "Request permission to come on the bridge!"

Casey motioned him up. "Chief, you've taught torpedo classes. What do you think about the exploder in the Mark XIV?"

"Sir, I've never seen one. It's classified."

"Do you think you could take one apart if you had one in your hands?"

"Yes, sir, but I'd have to finish the job in the brig."

"Don't worry. I just declassified it. Yeo will cut a stencil authorizing you to disassemble one and give your opinion of what's wrong with it."

Casey's discouragement soon dissolved in the vigor of his natural optimism. He circulated through the crew's quarters and spent some time in the torpedo rooms. "Figure on having some real live fish in here soon," he told Keith's watch. "The Navy accidentally makes a few good torpedoes, and we're going to have them aboard next time."

Scobie said despondently: "Hope so, Captain. Beginning to think we've got a jinx aboard."

"Now, who would that be?"

Scobie hesitated. "Mister Ratkowski. I hear he had a boat shot out from under him last time out."

"You call that bad luck? To be the sole survivor?"

"Ain't it better luck not to lose a boat at all?"

"What would you say to having *two* sole survivors aboard? Stocker swam away from a freighter last winter. That begins to sound like we're blessed, doesn't it?"

Scobie grinned.

"How're you coming with that exploder?" the captain asked Jolley, whose bunk was littered with morsels of brass and stainless steel.

"She's comin'. I don't know how they could turn out a thing with all these parts, though, and expect it to function when it hits a steel wall at fifty knots!"

"Maybe we can work out our own exploder—something based on a twenty-millimeter shell mounted backwards with a bolt against the fuse. What do you think?"

"Might work. Is that an order?"

"Sure, that's an order. Put the old exploder in a weighted bag and deep-six it. Next time we fire, shoot our retread last. That way we'll know if it works."

Around 2100 *Mako* surfaced and ran. The hissing of air into the buoyancy tanks woke Keith. The torpedo room was as hot and damp as a shower stall. His eyelids felt swollen and his brain was still drugged. Up in the maze of tubing a single light burned. It seemed to him that the sub limped a little, that the throbbing of her diesels was uneven—as if going home with nine torpedoes aboard was not her idea of a prideful thing to do. But it was suicidal, also, to engage the enemy with no more than a four-inch deck gun.

Pharmacist's Mate Mettick came through, wakening the crewmen who had watches coming up. "Hit the deck, Stocker!" Keith sat up and scratched his chest, then dropped to the deck and groped for his shoes. Just then the soft chiming of Battle Stations sounded. Someone lunged for the light switch. The lights came on brilliantly.

The main circuit crackled. "Now, hear this! This is the captain. It's just come to my attention that today is October 27, Navy Day!"

There was a dead silence. "Now, that ain't like the captain!" Hartman complained. "Wake the ship up for something like that."

"It's traditional to do something important on Navy Day—sink a warship, for example. By a happy coincidence, we have just sighted a cruiser in Kolima Bay. We're off the west coast of Bougainville Island. Intelligence tells us a wounded cruiser holed up somewhere along this coast after a brawl with our bombers last week. The chances are he's barely operational. It should be no problem to finish him off."

From the lookout's perch Keith saw a moonlit coast of mud and mangroves. He could smell the rotting filth of the jungle. The stars flickered as if blown upon, and a big slice of moon, like cake frosting, illuminated the harbor they were approaching. It had rained an hour before and clouds were still massed around the horizon.

The range was about six thousand yards. Kolima Bay was a shallow scoop in the coastline of Bougainville Island, only a mile across and with a wide mouth to guard. Back and forth across this entrance charged three destroyers, angrily warning off prowling surface craft. The cruiser was outlined against a white shell beach, a huge mail-fisted ship as large as some battleships. It was armed with torpedoes, eight-inch guns, dozens of smaller guns, and depth charges.

But this cruiser was in trouble. It had settled deeply by the bow and much of its stern was out of water. The massive superstructure—gun housings, battery director, signal bridge—was torn and twisted by bomb hits. Keith and the other forward lookout reported acetylene torches glowing like fireflies on the ship as the Japanese fought to repair the damage sufficiently to move it to a safe harbor.

Radar kept the ranges coming, while the officers on the bridge studied the patrol patterns of the destroyers. Torpedo crews stood by, fore and aft. But no one knew what sort of attack was in Captain Casey's mind. He was taciturn and more than ordinarily painstaking.

"Check your speeds again, Mister Ratkowski. I don't want one of those tin cans throwing a block when we begin to fire."

Radar reported: "Eighteen knots for the two ships closest to shore, Captain. Twenty-two for the other."

"Good. Open the outer doors. Stand by forward. Range—mark!"

"Three eight double oh."

Lieutenant Ramage, at the TDC, said: "Set!"

"Bearing—mark!"

"Zero four five."

"Set!"

Suddenly the little blue-green fireflies in the cruiser's superstructure began to wink out. Keith and the other lookout sounded off at the same moment. "They've picked us up!"

Casey shouted in a brawling voice: "*Fire!*"

The lurch of the ship made Keith grab at the rail. He saw the wake running out straight as an arrow. "Fire—fire—fire!" Casey emptied the forward tubes and ordered the helmsman to reverse course. He emptied the after tubes and ordered emergency speed and a dive to periscope depth. The destroyers were swinging seaward with searchlights slashing at the water. Casey manned the night periscope in the control room and waited.

"About that time," Mister Ramage said grimly.

Staring at stopwatches, they waited. Two minutes, and now only Casey's remodel could have failed to reach the target. A torpedo which missed the ship would explode on the beach; but the sonarman had detected no explosions.

WHAM!

The explosion rocked *Mako*.

"Right where the skin's thin!" Casey shouted. "He's on fire."

They ran for the open sea. Casey would sweep around the sea with the 'scope and come back to watch the cruiser. Unless they actually saw him go down, it could not be counted a sinking. Then another explosion rocked the big warship, almost deafening the sound operator. An ammunition compartment had been exploded by the flames. One after the other, additional explosions ripped the vitals from the cruiser.

"There he goes!"

They heard rumblings and muffled reports of exploding ammunition. *Mako* had won a fourth Japanese flag for her cockscomb. Out where the water was deep, Casey secured the ship for silent running, and the submarine slipped away through the dark jungles of the sea.

22

A half-day east of the Solomons, Radio Pearl ordered the boat south to Brisbane, Australia, where a new submarine base was equipped to supply the boats attached to Task Force 42. Subs which had been slugging it out in the Solomons and the Bismarcks were now saved the long runs back to Pearl Harbor and Midway.

The crew's reactions were mixed. Like base runners, they felt it would be nice to touch home plate before going out on patrol again. But men who had been in Brisbane before the war said it was a good liberty port, and the "Aussies" were much like Americans.

They cruised up the Brisbane River to the submarine base, where a relief crew took over *Mako* and all hands were given two weeks' liberty. Though it was early winter at home, it was summer in Brisbane. The air was hot and sultry. Keith, Hector, Hartman, and two other men hired a taxi and drove into the city. A smell of charcoal smoke, plus something uneven about the taxi's engine noises, aroused Keith's curiosity.

"What's this car run on?" he asked the driver.

"Charcoal, matey. We've got no petrol here."

"Petrol?"

"Gasoline, matey. I've got a charcoal burner aft. It heats charcoal in a tank, and the gas it gives off burns just like petrol."

Hartman muttered: "You think that's bad? Wait'll you eat Aussie steak."

"What's wrong with it?"

"It's mutton."

"What's mutton?"

"Mutton is sheep that's old enough to have a driver's license."

They skirted a plaza with dense groves of magnolia and banyan trees. It was sweet with flower fragrances. The city reminded Keith of a large southwestern town; it had that hot country look. Wide marquees and metal awnings shaded the sidewalks, where there were more United States sailors and Marines in view than Aussie servicemen. The driver said nearly all the Aussies were in Africa fighting Rommel.

"Well, here we are. Best temperance hotel in town!"

At the desk, they were given religious tracts, warned against liquor and cards, and sent up to a dingy room from which they could hear the jangling noises of the railroad yards. Keith could not sleep. Though he was used to heat and noise, the bed was too large and the noises were wrong. Once he found himself on the floor groping around for his shoes. In the semidarkness, Hartman was also hunting clothes.

"Knock it off," Hec groaned from his cot. "That was a church chime, not battle stations."

They went to an American movie the next afternoon, but left early. It was hard to sit still for two hours. Some Aussie soldiers took them to the USO. The Australians were colorful fighting men with trousers tucked into combat boots, large sombrero-type hats pinned up on one side, and an ostrich feather tucked into the ribbon. There were plenty of soft drinks, and even a southern-hemisphere version of an American malted milk. They danced with the healthy, pretty Australian girls, and everyone was singing a tune called, "Bless 'Em All." Another Australian song got less of a play. It was called "The Last Trip of the Old Ship."

After two days of time-killing, Keith realized that what he needed was exercise. Aboard ship there was virtually none. He looked disconsolately out the hotel window at the brown river winding to the sea. All at once he knew what he wanted. He tore into his seabag for a pair of exercise shorts.

On his cot, Hartman lowered a newspaper he had

been reading and watched him. "What's up, Sand-blower?"

"Going swimming!"

"Swimming? Where?"

"The river! Get your exercise shorts."

Hartman smiled. "I'll read you a little item from the paper. 'Bathers are warned against swimming in the river until further notice. Man-eating sharks have returned to local waters and only beaches protected by shark nets may be considered safe.' —Got any other ideas?" he asked.

Keith wandered back to the window. Then he turned again. "Where *can* you swim, then?"

"Ask a taxi driver."

Keith asked a cabbie, who said the best beach was fifteen miles from town, at a resort called Moonlight Beach.

"It's sort of a camp. There's beach cottages where you can do your own cooking on a gasoline stove. Some people like to goggle-fish there."

"Goggle-fish!"

"Aye, there's worlds of beautiful fish at Moonlight."

"Where can I get goggles?"

"People make their own, matey. They're shaped like masks. Some use redwood. The best, they say, are made out of old tires."

Keith bypassed the slow elevator and ran upstairs.

"Toro! Throw your skivvies in a bag and let's go."

"Where to?"

Keith took a deep breath, feeling his body sinking into the warm water. "Moonlight Beach, matey. By way of a junkyard."

All the way out on the preposterous little Puffing Billy of a train they worked on their faceplates. The junkman had cut sections from a tire for them, like slices through a garden hose, and from a shattered plate glass windshield he helped them cut circular plates. With wire, they locked the glass inside the circle of the rubber.

"I didn't know you were a goggler," Keith said, as the train rattled through the country.

"I ain't. But I was a lifeguard a couple of summers."

At Moonlight Beach they rented a sand-floored palm shack and sat in the sun to complete their masks. When they had fitted the masks so that they did not leak, they walked up the beach to a rocky point that ran out into the water. From experience Keith knew this was where the fish would be. Only stingrays and a few small surf fish inhabited the sandy areas. He swam out along the reef, gazing down at the weeds swaying gracefully from the sand, at the clean margin of the rocks where they rose toward the surface. A school of tiny yellow-and-black tropical fish came up and shimmered all around him like butterflies. Though there were hundreds of them within inches, not a single fin so much as touched him. A big lugger of an angelfish, black margined with iridescent blue and yellow, cruised up to look at him, and pouted with its round mouth. An eel did figure eights in the weeds below him, searching restlessly. A long blue-and-silver fish sped by. He could see a crab moving jerkily over a craggy rock. A nudibranch resembling an orange and purple butterfly fluttered past. He caught it in his hand and raised it above the water; it became a soggy little puddle of colored tendrils. He replaced it in the water and it fluttered away.

A rattling noise startled him. The words *Sonar contact!* formed in his head. It was exactly like the sound of a small, light motorboat cruising toward him. Finally, down in a cobbled bowl, he saw two moon-shaped triggerfish. He swam to within a few feet of them. They stared at him. The fluttering stopped. He could see tiny fins quivering at either side of their gills. The fluttering recommenced and now the fins were moving so fast he could scarcely see them.

Toro swam by, his black butch-cut head swiveling as he looked at everything. He was grinning foolishly, too entranced by it all to think clearly. At last they went up. Toro said the three words men would probably be saying centuries hence when they had their first glimpse of the underwater world:

"It's another world!"

Then they began asking each other, "Did you see—?" and, "Did you see—?" and, "Did you see —?" until they could stay away no longer and had to dive again.

Tired, they ate a light supper and lay on the still-warm sand looking up at the southern stars. Far away some campers were singing in harmony, "Bless 'Em All."

"Makes you feel guilty," Keith said.

"About what?"

"Being here, when the dogfaces are dying in the mud back in the Solomons."

"Don't ever feel guilty about liberty, Sandblower," the quartermaster said gently. "So what if we eat good, don't sleep in the mud, and get a few days' liberty when we finish a patrol? When our luck sours, we don't just lose a few men. We get wiped out."

"I guess you're right."

"And nobody ever knows how. 'Missing, presumed lost.' That's how they chalk it up. Even the ships we torpedo are better off than us. Maybe they save half the crew. But there ain't many that walk out of a depth charging like Mister Ratkowski did."

"Uh-huh."

"You know what they say in the Coast Guard?"

Toro recalled. " 'You have to go out. You don't have to come back.' "

They maintained a thoughtful silence.

"Crazy hobby for a submariner, ain't it?" Toro said at last.

"What's that?"

"Playing with fish. When the chances are you'n me will wind up locked in a submarine till the oceans go dry. We'll get our fill of fish then, good buddy!"

The two weeks melted away. Keith and Toro enticed other *Mako* men out to the beach, and Moonlight began to resemble boot camp. Keith went down to the sub base once and looked at *Mako*. She was being scraped clean of grass and barnacles and repainted. A more efficient radar head had been installed. Tons of supplies were being taken aboard.

The Brisbane papers told of a tremendous sea battle between U.S. ships and a heavy-muscled Japanese armada. They fought around the clock, and eight or nine more ships joined the silent fleet at the bottom of Ironbottom Sound. The Americans suffered heavily. Only a day later, eleven Japanese transports full of troops tried to bull their way through to Guadalcanal. American planes and ships attacked them and their escorts, sinking seven of the transports. The other four unloaded a few thousand troops, but were sunk on the beach before they could set down supplies.

They called it a great victory. But the submariners wondered whether it was like Pyrrhus's costly victory over the Romans: *"One more such victory, and we are utterly undone!"* The swollen bodies of nearly two thousand American fighting men now floated in the waters of the Solomons, while other thousands were dying ashore.

23

A band came down to the dock and played while *Mako* went back to war. The lines were singled up, the diesels coughed and sputtered, and the brow was pushed in. With a blast of her whistle, she said good-bye to the group of girls and Navy men on the dock.

"You have to go out. You don't have to come back."

On deck with the channel watch, Keith thought about the saying as they cruised down the river. Land thoughts and land feelings broke with the bowline. They were submariners again, creatures who lived in a bottle which could be shattered; soft-bodied creatures like the hermit crab, which sought a hard shell for armor and was helpless without it.

Maybe the dogfaces had the best of it: they saw the enemy, heard him scream in anger, screamed back in anger, and killed in anger. A submariner killed cold-bloodedly by slide rule, burned his victims in gasoline, cooked them in live steam, shredded them with knife-edged fragments of their own ships.

The channel watch was secured. All hands went belowdecks except the bridge watch and lookouts. In the messroom, Soper had dishpans of sandwiches on the tables in lieu of an ordinary lunch. The sandwiches were dry and curled. Keith shrugged and began to eat. But Mettick suddenly screamed at the cook,

"Is *this* what you call lunch?"

"That's what you're gettin' for lunch!" Soper shouted back. "I got work to do."

"You don't say!" Mettick sneered. "Cutting pictures out of movie magazines?"

"I've got to rearrange all my stores. Them jokers didn't put my flour in the freeze locker."

"Why should they?"

"You want your bread with weevils next week? It's all the same to me, swabbie."

He paused in his work to put a record on a phonograph he had brought aboard. The tune was familiar; suddenly Hartman remembered it. He leaped up and roared:

"Take that record off, you idiot!"

"I like it," Soper said, smiling blandly.

"What's the matter with it?" Keith asked Toro.

"It's that Aussie song, 'The Last Trip of the Old Ship'! You want to jinx the boat?"

The cook started the record over when it had finished. Hartman took his sandwiches and coffee and went aft. Two or three other small arguments were in progress. Somebody was angry at Hec for trying to use captured Japanese occupation currency in a card game, and someone else was lecturing a mate who had forgotten to mail a letter for him.

The change from landlubber to killer, Keith began to realize, was a painful process.

Mako boomed sturdily north through the Coral Sea. She kept the Solomons to starboard while heading for the Bismarck Archipelago. Off New Britain a small tanker was sighted and they put three torpedoes into her. All three exploded, and the ship went down in ninety seconds.

"We done it! We done it!" yelled Becket from the sonar console.

Casey was sweating and beaming as he turned the periscope over to the exec. "We *did* it," he corrected with a grin.

"We sure did, Cap'm!"

"And we just happen to be firing good torpedoes this time. We've got a load of Mark X's aboard. They may be as old-fashioned as a tea kettle, but they're just as reliable. I refused to take more Mark XIV's."

A couple of days later they crossed the Equator and the captain made an announcement. "We're going on up to the Palau Islands and find out where all that shipping is that we hear about. Intelligence is that the Japs have major naval and merchant shipping going in and out of the Palaus. We've reconnoitered it by sub but haven't contacted anything. This doesn't make sense, because the Palaus are barricaded by coral reefs, and the only practical way in is Malakal Passage, where we're heading."

They went on station off Malakal Passage, in the southeast coral barrier of the island group. The sea had the oily shimmer of an undulating piece of gray silk, while the pale sun poured down a leaden heat. Trying to penetrate the gauzy haze that rose from the sea, the lookouts' eyes ached after a half-hour's watch. Belowdecks the heat kept building. In the crew's mess Soper played "The Last Trip of the Old Ship."

The feeling of expectancy began to dull. A week passed, and nothing but occasional blurs of smoke were sighted. Hull down, these ships escaped before *Mako* could overtake them. The only change was in the weather. Frequent rain squalls blew up, drenched the islands and lashed the sea, and gave way to white, blistering heat.

Once a large sampan passed within two miles. Casey secured for silent running and watched it pass unmolested under a cloud of greasy smoke, plowing a vanishing furrow on a flat sea. They were after the big targets—the convoys. The captain grew tense and irritable.

"There's something fishy about this deal! We *know* ships are coming down from Japan and the Philippines. They've got to refuel and transship somewhere. It's *got* to be here. But where are they?"

"Maybe Truk Island still handles all the traffic," the exec suggested.

"Nuts! Truk's been practically isolated for weeks. Nossir! A lot of big ships are making port here."

The days dragged on. The crew was restless. Standing lookout watches. Listening at the sonar gear. Drinking coffee. Nothing more exciting than watching little fishing boats pass. Sleeping. The skipper looked strained and tired. He slept on a cot in the conning tower, always on hair trigger. Suddenly, one day, he rose with a lurch.

"Sound! Whereaway?" he shouted.

The conning tower watch blinked at him. Casey sagged. He sat down and rubbed his face briskly. "Wake up, boy!" he muttered. "I thought we'd contacted something. Sound, what do you hear?"

Keith had turned up the volume to bring in a new noise. He sat back. "Just a lot of small reef fish."

"Any other fish sounds?"

"No, sir, nothing big."

The skipper looked thoughtful. "Mister Ratkowski, let's have the log."

Casey thumbed through the book. " '. . . Large sampan. Small sampan. Native boat, unidentified. Two sampans.' " He stared sourly at the exec. "I thought you were supposed to be a hotshot navigator. I don't think we're anywhere near Malakal Passage!"

155

"Got to be, Captain! I've taken sun shots and moon shots and star shots. We're three miles west of Malakal Passage. Hell, you can see the beach!"

"What do the charts say about the depths here?"

"Deep enough for navy ships, even."

"Then how come," Casey charged, "nothing bigger than five hundred tons goes through here? How come we're getting small fish sounds?"

The exec looked at him blankly.

"I'll check," he said suddenly.

He went up to the bridge. Returning, he worked with charts, almanacs and calipers. "Captain, unless I've lost my mind we've *got* to be in Malakal Passage!"

"Let's take a single ping for depth," Casey said.

The fathometer, trapping the ping as it bounced back from the ocean floor, showed twenty fathoms: about a hundred and twenty feet. "Deep water, eh?" Casey said with a tight grin. "What's the chart show?"

Ratkowski squinted at the tiny, flyspeck figures which gave him the depths on the charts. "Nothing under three hundred feet!"

"Let's drift into the passage and see how it looks," Casey said suddenly.

They cruised a few miles into the coral barrier, but came to an emergency stop as the water suddenly shoaled dangerously. "No naval ships have gone through *this* channel, mister," Casey said grimly. "Let's head north and find the channel they're really using!"

Ignoring the charts, they probed at the western coral barrier. Within a ring of coral reefs the low-lying Palaus showed their ragged hoods of jungle growth. Again and again, they had to forget caution and use the fathometer, which might betray them with its pinging. Midway up the western side of the island group, however, the water suddenly deepened.

"Where are we?" Casey swept the hot gray sea with the periscope.

"The chart calls it Toagel Mlungui Passage. Average depth too shallow for anything large."

"Throw it away!" Casey snorted. Then, "Wait a minute! Wait a minute! Bring her up to clear the radar head. Radar, see if that's smoke or clouds at about three five zero."

The green and amber cathodes glowed. The normal "grass-like" fuzziness covered the scope, but almost immediately the sweeping arm began bringing up bright points of luminescence. The islands were plainly discernible. To the northwest, small pips burned on the sensitized glass a few miles seaward.

"Convoy at three four five! Range eleven thousand! Four, five—*six ships!*"

24

"Radio Pearl from *Mako*, I have an urgent message. Radio Pearl from *Mako*, I have an urgent message. . . ."

Casey sent the frantic dispatch while they waited for the convoy to come within torpedo range. A procedure sign came back immediately which signified: "Go ahead, we're ready."

"From *Mako* to ComSubPac and all submarines in Marianas-Carolines area. Am engaging convoy six ships entering Toagel Mlungui Channel in Palau Islands. Disregard charts. Malakal Passage too shallow for deep-draft ships."

From smoke, the first ship grew to masts, then to the superstructure of a big tanker. A half-mile to the tanker's port steamed another tanker with heavy guns fore and aft. The six ships were in two columns led by three big tankers, with three freighters following. Being so close to safety, they were not even zigging. While the plotting party sweated, the submarine lay to a mile and a half south of the convoy. Black storm clouds towered beyond the ships, slashed by dazzling knives of lightning.

"Heavy screws at zero three five!" Keith sang out.

Casey swiveled the 'scope. "Uh-huh! A destroyer to welcome them home. Plot, let's have a course to take him out of action." He flipped his thumbs and the 'scope slid down into the well.

Keith heard the strong *chug* of the cargo vessels cut across by the arrogant *chow-chow-chow* of the destroyer rushing to meet them. Recognition signals flashed from tanker to destroyer and back. In the conning tower, the attack team sweated over its problems.

"Give it fifteen feet depth. Estimated speed eighteen knots. Course two six four."

"Set!"

"Range, two oh double oh yards."

"Set!"

"Stand by forward."

Now came the preattack silence and tension, the heat mounting unbearably, to one hundred and twenty-two degrees in the conning tower—probably a hundred and thirty in the engine room. In the messroom, a few men with nearby stations nibbled toast and coffee, setting the mugs down carefully to avoid making the slightest sound. A motor mach with heavy shoes plodded forward for a cup of coffee and was threatened by his off-watch mates. He pulled off his shoes and tiptoed. The man wearing the battle phones told his grim bedtime story to men about to kill or die.

"On the firing bearing, Captain."

"Fire One! Fire Two! Fire Three!"

The firing key operator repeated the torpedo officer's commands as he pressed the key. A spread of three torpedoes raced out at ten-second intervals. Their tracks, long, pale stripes on the surface of the water, were perfectly visible. Almost at once there was a change in the speed and pitch of the destroyer's screws. The fish had been sighted.

"He's turning toward us, Captain!" Keith reported.

Boom! A shell landed close to the periscope and Casey ducked. He laughed and again pushed his forehead against the cushion. "They're running true. First one's passing forward. Second one's going to be close. Third may be amidships."

WHAM! WHAM!

Shock waves rocked *Mako.* Light globes swung on the stubby extensions Casey had had rigged up for depth charge situations.

"Two hits!" he shouted. "We broke him in half!"

The same ghastly breaking-up noises came from the sound gear. Keith shuddered. Through the hull the whole crew could hear other explosions. There was no time to exult and take turns looking through the periscope.

"Start tracking the first AO!"

But now the ships were all zigging. Sooty clouds

erupted from their stacks, rising thick and black against the mountainous storm clouds moving closer. The big attack oiler went sharp left, trying to run. But at the same time, the ship leading the second column came hard right and zigged toward the first. The two *marus* headed for a collision—the kind of situation the Old Man knew how to play like a poker hand. Blinkers flashed wildly aboard the Japanese ships.

Casey set up a torpedo track which anticipated that the near ship would swing right to avoid the other ship. "Stand by forward! He's coming around!"

"Let's shoot! The solution checks, Captain!"

"Fire Four! Fire Five! Check fire. Shift targets to second ship."

Casey put the boat over a few degrees to gain a new setup on the second tanker, which, as he had anticipated, had turned left to avoid colliding with the other. Course, bearing, and speed were cranked into the TDC. Meanwhile, the seconds ticked off.

The first fish were still racing toward the first *maru. Mako* had an embarrassment of targets, and had already spent three of her six forward torpedoes on the destroyer. Two more had been fired at the first tanker, and a single fish remained to hurl at the second.

"Fire Six! *Right* full rudder—all ahead full. Stand by aft!"

Mako heeled lightly as the helmsman swung his

wheel hard. Pivoting to present her stern tubes, she leaned into the turn, responsive and eager as a war-horse.

"A hit!" Casey roared. "Holy cow! It's a gasoline tanker!"

He turned from the 'scope, rubbing his eyes. The ship had burst into incandescence like a flash bulb as the searing white flame soared into the air. Six million gallons of aviation gasoline had exploded all at once, cremating the men who had brought the ship all the way from Japan or Singapore.

"Come to radar depth! Radar, watch for ships and aircraft from Palau. Mister Ratkowski, let's take that last tanker next. Lord above, it's a circus up there!"

A numbing shock wave caught them with rocking, jolting force. A man staggered and almost fell into the periscope well. The exec caught his arm, clinging with his free hand to a valve anchored to the bulkhead. Casey wheeled the periscope around. A second explosion hammered at them. Then a third and fourth wave hit so hard that helmsman and planesmen had to fight the wheels to keep her on course and depth. Keith heard sizzling sounds, booming sounds, grinding of machinery, and then a vast explosion. Picturing the red horror above, he felt weak and sick.

"Ammo ship! *Brother!* We've *got* to get a camera on this boat. I never saw anything so—Mister, take a look!"

The exec glanced quickly through the periscope and returned it to the captain with a shudder. "She's red-hot from stem to stern," he said with a grimace. "Captain, we'd better make our play for the other AO and take off. We're only a few minutes by air from the field at Peleliu."

"Take off! We're going to sink this whole convoy before we quit."

Keith glanced around. Hartman met his eyes. *Please, God, let's get out of here!* his face said. With a naval base only a short distance away, they were in imminent danger of air attack.

"We've only got four fish in the tubes," Ratkowski pleaded, "and there's three ships left!"

"Bearing on that tanker—mark! Range—mark! Set gyros ten feet. Make speed ten knots. How's that for the TDC, Mister Ramage?"

His red tee shirt plastered to his torso, Lieutenant Ramage replied: "All set!"

"Coming on the firing bearing!"

"Stand by aft—he's zigged. New target course. Make speed eleven knots. Final firing bearing— Fire!" With a hiss of air and the sudden whine of gears, the torpedoes lurched out. The phones scraped and rattled with the chaos in the blazing sea outside *Mako's* hull. Pressure increased in the boat as the compressed air which launched the fish piled pound on pound against the eardrums.

"The tubs are all over the place!" Casey exulted.

"They're going crazy. Wait a minute—there's one trying to make the channel."

In a fighting, furious voice, he tracked the ship. He had an instinct for predicting which way a scared ship's captain would turn and how long he would stay on that tack, as though he could measure his fear and daring. In a cold recess of his mind, he made calculations based on these guesses and snapped the results at his exec, who checked them with the Is-Was and relayed them to the gunnery officer.

Radar sang out: "Aircraft at twelve thousand yards, one two zero degrees relative!"

"Rig for depth charge!"

Another explosion shook the sea. Another hit. A hundred men, more or less, hurled burned and bleeding into the ocean. The water was foul with oil and blood; it boiled from the white-hot iron thrust into it. Ten thousand fish killed by the explosions would float belly up, while long, ghostlike sharks followed the tendrils of blood into the area.

Four down and two to go.

"Aircraft at seven five double oh!"

Taking his last bearings on the freighter, the skipper decided that it would not make another zig: it was running like a scared rabbit for the channel.

"Fire Nine! Fire Ten! Left ten degrees rudder—all ahead emergency! Pull the plug."

Before *Mako* had gone deep, the first torpedo shook the sea like a rug and the submarine faltered. Another hit! Five down and one to go. Diving at full power, she chewed green water all the way down. In the conning tower, everyone clung to something. They could not hear the dive bomber which had been sent out to kill the boat; but they knew that, behind plastic goggles, keen eyes were seeking them.

"Sound! Bearing on that rain squall!"

Keith twisted the sound crank over the area where the black storm clouds had been moving in. He heard rain hissing on the water and passed the bearing to the captain. Casey changed course a few degrees, calling for full power as they raced for the cover of the rain squall where even radar would not be able to detect them after they resurfaced. Then there was a splash in the sound phones, and Keith yanked them off an instant before the first aerial bomb exploded.

Wrenched by the detonation, the sub went dark. Someone cut on the emergency lamps. Another bomb exploded farther forward and tipped the boat sharply down by the bow. *Mako*'s dive was suddenly a headlong angle for the bottom. Gear chimed and crashed on the deck. Everyone seemed to be on his knees scrambling for a handhold as they all slid forward. The hand on the big clocklike depth gauge hit a hundred and fifty feet and passed it at a run.

"All back emergency! Hard rudder left! Blow the forward group!"

The captain was fighting now to bring her out of the dive, which might end on the bottom. Someone reached the engine room telegraph and swung it hard to alert the maneuvering room. Bells rang, and the boat shuddered as the screws went to reverse. Another bomb exploded and *Mako* seemed to drop into a hole blasted in the water, the angle of her descent increasing even more. Keith watched the shallow depth gauge spinning like a runaway clock. Creaking and groaning, the submarine passed two hundred feet, two twenty-five, two fifty.

"Bow planes are locked, sir!" Hartman shouted.

The executive officer got on the big wheel with him and they tried to force it around. They could not budge the wheel, and the big steel fins partially controlling their angle of descent continued to force *Mako* into the deeper water.

"Back, blow and pray!" the captain panted.

Someone hit the fathometer button and the ping came back from the coral bottom to read, *Two hundred feet*. Only two hundred feet between them and the coral. . . . A cavernous quiet came, broken by the steady clanging of loose objects on the deck. Keith could feel the heavy water pressing against the hull, heard the ship's metal plates popping as they gave under the pressure. Leaks were reported in the antenna trunk and the forward torpedo room, now the deepest part of the boat by perhaps a hundred feet.

"Make her squat, Mister Bratton!" Casey bawled down to the diving officer. Bratton flooded everything aft. Gradually the stern began to settle. The screws got hold of the water and pulled the boat back a little. Just then a leak started in the conning tower and a stream of water a quarter-inch thick showered the compartment. All at once the bow planes broke loose. Hartman and Ratkowski both stumbled away and bounced off a bulkhead. Toro dived for the wheel and put his strength and weight into the struggle.

The boat leveled off. "Blow everything!" Casey shouted. Someone tried to clamp his hand over the leak in the bulkhead, but the stream slapped it away. Once she started up, *Mako* rose fast. Keith listened for the rain squall again as she came back on course at two hundred feet. Ratkowski, tallow-white, became ill and asked for relief.

The boat stole into the protection of the storm. Damage-control parties went to work. Rocking silently on the rain-whipped water, they listened for the enemy. Torpedo tubes were being reloaded. Watches had been relieved, and Keith was in the messroom eating a sandwich. The captain came down to the crew's mess for a cup of coffee and a sandwich, eating in a hungry, preoccupied silence.

"Find out whether we've got fish in the tubes yet, will you?"

Becket phoned. "Tubes ready aft. Four down and two to go, forward."

"I want to congratulate you men," Casey said finally, looking around. "All compartments kept their heads. One slip and we'd have stayed down for the second show."

"We sure picked the lock on the Japs' door, huh?" Becket chuckled. "It's funny they could have been sneaking in only seventeen miles north and nobody even seen them. Too bad we didn't make a clean sweep, huh, Captain?"

Casey began to grin. "Where do you get that 'didn't' stuff?"

Becket's grin faded. The compartment seemed to become clammy. "I don't get you, sir."

"Sound will report if that AK tries to sneak back. Possibly he'll clear out, but I doubt it, this close to port. I promised you a clean sweep on this patrol, and I'm not going to let you down. I still think we can knock him off before they get any more tin cans on us. So all we've got to worry about is bombers."

Fear and excitement came back into Keith's mouth

with a taste of brass. His heart pounded as he remembered the bombs detonating. He looked at Hartman, who had been wiping his face with a towel. Toro lowered it and gazed blankly at the skipper.

Lieutenant Ramage ducked back from the control room. "Sound's picked something up, Captain."

"Good! Tell the C.O.B. to hurry up with those fish and we'll get under way."

25

Keith stood a messenger watch in the control room. All he could think of was bodies floating in the muck of oil and blood. The periscope was pushing through this garbage of human bodies as the boat prowled Toagel Mlungui Channel. At one-third speed, she crept toward her target, now visible on the horizon and making for the channel. He kept tasting his lunch and having to swallow collected saliva.

"Down 'scope," Casey said. "What a mess! There must be a couple of hundred Japs floating around on rafts, and I wouldn't guess how many live and dead ones in jackets."

A few airplanes had been hovering around, dropping life rafts to survivors and searching for the submarine. Casey held a discussion with the Chief Electrician's Mate.

"How's our power holding out? I'd like to bend on some speed, if we can do it without burning up our battery."

"We're running on a nearly flat can right now, Captain."

"Oh, come on. You can tease a little more out of it, can't you? It will be dark soon and we can charge."

"Well . . ." The chief grumbled, figured some more and decided they could risk full speed for a short time. "But if we get pinned down tonight, we'll have to break out the oars."

The freighter was zigging all over now, making one-minute zigs. Another bomber came out from the Peleliu airfield, and the boat went deep. When they returned to periscope depth, the plane was gone and the ship was in ideal firing range.

"Sound bearings!"

Becket chanted the bearings as they came closer.

"Stand by forward! Stand by One!" There were the usual clipped commands.

"Shoot!" Casey commanded. They fired a spread of three fish. A great geyser of debris and dirty water erupted under the stacks. The ship separated into halves. Hundreds of small splashes sparkled on the water as particles of wood and metal rained down. The second torpedo went home. On *Mako* the men held their breath, waiting. Then a more distant explosion traveled back through the water and jolted them.

Peering through the 'scope, Casey reported what he saw. "He's rolling over! There goes his boiler.

I don't see many survivors—most of them must've been below when it hit. We got 'em! *Clean sweep!*" he bawled.

Everyone was pounding everyone else on the back and yelling. *Clean sweep!* Someone pulled down the broom from the overhead and flourished it. Six ships in one day! Fifty thousand tons of shipping! The skipper composed a message as soon as they had cleared the area and could surface.

"Sighted six ships, sank same. Will hunt till we run out of targets."

ComSubPac radioed back: "Congratulations, Lou. Your picture is on the piano."

26

Twenty-four hours later, *Mako* sank a small attack
transport a hundred miles northwest of the Palaus.
Her torpedoes spent, she headed back to Brisbane.
The captain was jubilant.

"Mister Ratkowski, I'll bet we've set a record of
some kind! We may even sink a couple more on
the way to the barn."

"What with?"

"The deck gun. The gun crew needs practice anyway. I still say a submarine ought to have heavier
armament."

"And maybe a flight deck, too," Ratkowski said,
"and then they'd call us a carrier."

Casey laughed. "I guess I get carried away. Good
thing I've got you along to keep me out of trouble."

Midwatch, first watch, morning watch. The heat
building unbearably during the day; then the long
monotonous lookout watches of the night. The
alarms that sent the boat down with an almost
playful flash of her stern, and the exhilaration of

bursting back through the surface wet as a seal, in a bath of green bubbles. She was proud, and they were proud of her.

Off Guadalcanal, radar reported: "Radar contact!"

It was dark, a yellow paring of moon rising from beyond Guadalcanal. "What've you got?" the captain asked.

"Don't know, sir. It's pretty small."

They pressed toward the object, on the chance that it might be a life raft. Suddenly the port lookout bawled: "Flotsam dead ahead!"

"All back emergency!"

A rattling shudder shook the boat. To those on the bridge, the object looked like a sodden log. The chief went out on the bullnose to examine it by flashlight. Suddenly he gave a bellow of warning.

"*Torpedo!*"

Mako backed off and eyed the thing warily. Jolley came up to the bridge.

"One of ours?" Casey asked.

"Couldn't tell, sir! But if it's magnetic, it might decide to work all of a sudden. We better high-tail it out, Cap'm."

"We're out of range. If that's a Japanese torpedo, I'd sure like to take it home."

From the lookout's perch, Keith glanced down. Jolley's jaw sagged. "Great snakes, Captain! I hope you're kidding!"

"I'm serious. If we had an exploder like the Japs, this war would be over in no time. Here's our chance to copy it."

"Do you mean you want to tow it home?" the executive officer demanded.

"Wouldn't dare. I was thinking of lashing it onto the foredeck after we'd disarmed it. What do you think?"

"I think you're crazy," the exec replied.

"There wouldn't be any risk, once it was disarmed," the captain argued. "It's got to have a gizmo of some kind in the warhead that they turn to arm it. Now, if it were set back to neutral, it couldn't go off. Right?"

"If it operates the same as ours."

"Then we'll get a line onto it and drag it across the bottom. If it goes off, we won't be any worse than shook up. . . . I'll need volunteers," he said, "to paddle over in a raft and disarm it."

Jolley said, "You got your volunteer, Captain. I've been waitin' a long time for this."

"How long, Chief?"

"Six years. I took a class in foreign torpedoes at New London. If the Japs haven't changed their exploder, I'll have that fish lashed to the deck in no time at all."

"What'll you need?"

"A rubber boat and a few tools. And somebody to row the boat."

Keith cleared his throat. "Request permission to go with the C.O.B., Captain!"

Surprised, Chief Jolley glanced up. "Okay with me. I'll be waiting on the foredeck."

Wearing exercise shorts and life jackets, they rowed away in the rubber boat. The chief had brought a flashlight, crowbar, screwdriver, and hammer. They towed a heevey-line attached to a heavier towing line on the boat. *Mako* lay far astern. As he rowed, Keith felt the chief's eyes on him.

"Well, well!" said Jolley.

"Well what, Chief?"

"I always knew a kid who had the nerve to belt a chief couldn't be all bad. Disarming a dud torpedo takes guts, but I claim that took more."

"All it took was ignorance. If I'd known as much about the Navy then as I know now, I'd have transferred to Cooks and Bakers five minutes after I belted you."

They paddled around the torpedo looking for Japanese lettering. Only a portion of the warhead was fully above the water. When Jolley's paddle clashed against it, they flinched. They regarded it with the same tense respect one gives a boil which the doctor is about to lance. No large lettering was visible, and finally they slipped in close and examined the places where designations would have been stamped into the metal of a Stateside torpedo.

Keith ran his hand over the metal. It was slimy from long immersion, but as yet no grass or barnacles had taken hold.

"Give me the flashlight, Chief!"

Switching on the light, he leaned close to a line of characters stamped in the bronze. Then he sat back and switched off the light.

"Japanese!"

Jolley rubbed his hands together. "It's my baby, I guess. I hope they taught us right in that class!"

Slipping into the water, he began searching for the little arming propeller in the warhead. "Just like old times, eh? Remember that inboard slug you fired?"

Keith smiled nervously.

The chief kept talking while he ran his hands over the slimy bronze. "According to the Hague Convention, duds are supposed to sink within thirty minutes. Looks like this was a double dud—no shootee, no sinkee. Okay, I got it! Now, row off and wait for the signal."

"No use, Chief. It'd blow me a mile in the air anyway."

"That's right," Jolley agreed. "I just thought you might feel better."

He worked fast, with only a quiet gurgling of water around his arms as he moved. "I'm revolving the propeller backwards, now. That'll pull the detonator out of the exploder mechanism. Right? Okay.

What tool will I need to extract the exploder after it's disarmed, Stocker?"

"Screwdriver!" Keith responded.

"Hand it here."

He reached beneath the torpedo and worked blindly. Once Keith saw him looking up at the stars; but his eyes were closed. At last he began, with slow, cautious motions, to lower something from the warhead. All of a sudden he came stroking toward the raft. Reaching it, he dropped something bright and dripping on the floor. He crawled in and crouched on all fours for a full half-minute, trembling.

Then he looked up. "Make fast the heevey-line in the nose ring. She'll be starting to sink now. That there," he said, indicating the clocklike works in the bottom of the raft, "is a Jap exploder. What do you think of that? We got the captain his Japanese torpedo!"

They paddled back. Hot chocolate and doughnuts were waiting for them. The captain had the torpedo tied hard to a cable. Then, in shallow water, he dragged it over the coral heads to make sure it was disarmed. Afterward he had it towed in and made fast to the deck.

On a bright, hot morning they started up the Brisbane River to the submarine docks, a broomstick tied to the periscope shears. Over the ship's radio they listened to the war news. On Guadalcanal the Japanese were in bloody retreat. Shortages of food and supplies had crippled them. Another tremendous naval battle had made it clear that the Imperial Navy could no longer cross Ironbottom Sound except at great cost.

As they cruised past the big shade trees overhanging the riverbanks, girls in bathing suits waved at them from boats and rafts. Whistling and shouting, the maneuvering watch waved back. The lookouts put the glasses on them, and Hartman reported excitedly:

"They *look* like girls. . . . They *sound* like girls. . . . They *are* girls!"

"As you were," the deck officer ordered. "The watch has not been secured."

The paymaster and a mound of mail bags were waiting on the dock. Standing on the foredeck, Jolley bawled: "Mail Call!" and began handing out the letters. Keith had five letters from his aunt and uncle, and a couple of others which he had not time to inspect, as several cars pulled up on the dock. A group of Navy brass and some civilians encircled the captain. Jolley blew his whistle and the crew came to attention on deck. The captain was receiving an admiral's congratulations on having discovered the passage the Japanese were using into the Palau group. In the days since *Mako* had gone off station, thousands of tons of shipping had already been sunk and another main artery of Japan's lifeline had been tied off.

Casey got a medal, the boat's crew received a unit citation, and sheaves of tickets to moving picture theaters and dance halls were presented to the men. A reporter looked at the crew, neatly rigged out in liberty whites but still bearded and with a patina of deep-water wildness, and grinned:

"They look like a bunch of cut-throats, Admiral."

"Well, maybe corsairs," the admiral conceded.

"Corsairs. . . . Casey's Corsairs," the reporter said, and he wrote something on a thick fold of newsprint.

The officers departed in automobiles, and the crew was dismissed. A special ordnance detail moved in to take charge of the Japanese torpedo. A relief crew boarded the ship, and a line of workmen in steel helmets immediately started body and fender work and minor repairs. Keith, Toro, and some shipmates hired the same charcoal-burning taxicab and headed for town in a cloud of smoke.

In the cab, everyone was reading mail. In addition to the letters from his Aunt Julia, Keith had mail from his draft board and a girl at the University. At the bottom of the pile was a wrinkled envelope bearing the frank of the United States Army. It had been forwarded from so many old addresses that the envelope was disintegrating. He opened it, and drew out another envelope, even more wrinkled. Inside, there was a crisp note from a general he had never heard of.

"My dear Mr. Stocker: I am glad to be able to forward to you this letter, which your father wrote shortly before his death on Corregidor. Along with some other mail and a few survivors, it was brought out by submarine. Please accept the sincere . . ."

The words swam out of focus. He swallowed a lump in his throat. Putting the mail away, he gazed out the window. Suddenly he was sorry for many, many things that had happened between him and his father; sorry for just as many things that should have happened, and hadn't. He was sure his father had never quite understood him, a boy so different from himself; and probably he had not understood his father.

He put the letter in his pocket. Reaction from the long, brutal patrol, with its sleeplessness, punishment, and terrors, was rising in him. He wanted to put his back to the sea and the war and keep moving. He felt that whatever his father had had to say during his last hours of life might be too much for him.

27

That night they went to a USO dance. The Americans loved the Aussie girls. They were attractive and lively, in many ways just like the girls at home. A slim, dark-haired girl named Susan noticed Keith's dolphins while they were dancing.

"You're a submariner, aren't you?"

"Yes, but let's talk about you. I can always talk submarines."

"Well, I can't, Yank. And if you're just in from a war patrol, you must be one of Casey's Corsairs."

Keith looked at her. "Casey's *what?* Where did you pick that up?"

"The newspapers, silly. The papers say that Casey's Corsairs have just come back from a record-making patrol. And that you sank ninety thousand tons of enemy shipping."

"Dream on!" Keith laughed. "It was more like forty."

Her eyes sparkled. He was not certain whether he was being teased or not.

"No, really. We're expecting big things of Captain Casey and his crew," she assured him.

"I hope we won't let you down. It would be an awful disappointment to take a torpedo amidships, with everyone counting on us."

It was late when they returned to the dismal little hotel with its damp heat. He stripped to his shorts and lay on the cot. After a moment he looked over at Hartman. "Hey, Toro!"

"Huh?" Toro yawned.

"What about Moonlight Beach tomorrow?"

"Gimme another day at the hog trough, kid. Then I'm your man."

Two mornings later, they took the puffing little train out to the resort and rented a palm shack. There had been a shark scare, and only a few people were in the water.

"I don't know," Toro said dubiously, watching the ranks of waves marching in. "What makes us any more immune to sharks than the next guy?"

"I figure like this: how many people have been killed by sharks, compared to the number of submariners that went out and didn't come back?"

"A lot of steeplejacks get killed, too, plus a lot of guys that ride motorcycles. But it don't prolong a steeplejack's life to ride a motorcycle to work, does it?"

Keith shrugged. "I don't believe sharks are as

dangerous as people think, anyway. I've seen dozens of them. They feed on garbage and crippled fish at the surface. Just don't thrash around at the surface if you see one, and you're all right."

"It would be just my luck that the shark would think *I* looked like garbage."

Out of prudence, they stayed in fairly shallow water, where there were many coral heads to deter big fish like sharks. The warm water glittered with hundreds of jewellike tropicals. Rainbow-tinted anemones glowed on the bottom, and scarlet lichens burned on the shady sides of the rocks. Keith sighed, letting the peace and beauty of it enfold him. The blood-letting and the shattering terror of depth charges seemed ages away.

With big plans for a fish fry, Toro had borrowed a clumsy wooden spear with a three-pronged steel point. Keith had forgotten about him, until abruptly he heard a solid *thunk!* behind him. He twisted and saw the silver flash of a struggling fish. Toro had driven the spear into the back of a steel-blue fish about twenty inches long. The fish was strong, and Toro was hauled from side to side, unable to bring it up. Excited by the contest, smaller fish darted through the cloud of blood spilling from the wound in the back of the fish. Pity for the fish impaled on the spear clutched at Keith.

Suddenly Hartman twisted, grimacing and thrusting the spear handle at him. He was winded, and wanted time to swim up and get his breath. With an involuntary stiffening, Keith accepted the spear.

The big blue fish was making croaking sounds with its air sacs. In its neat, symmetrical beauty there was great strength, but the wound in the smooth black armor had torn wider. The blood was spilling out profusely, clouding the water like red dust. Pain was in its struggling, too; pain and fear came up the spear handle in the frantic, quivering vibrations.

Keith looked for Toro, but he was still resting on the surface. Then he looked at the clean-lined de-lineation of loveliness impaled on the spear: beauty in its death throes. He knew he had to put an end to the suffering. Setting his teeth, he placed his feet against the fish on either side of the wound and managed to tear the point out. The fish flopped onto its side and swam in a tight circle above the weed. Keith waited and then drove the point into its head. It stopped struggling almost at once.

Toro came down, grinning when he saw that the fish was finished. It was a fine one, a real prize. Keith relinquished the spear and swam in. Once he heard Toro yell, but he kept going.

In the warm night, they sat on the beach. "It's not that there's anything wrong with fishing or hunting," he said after supper. "We have to have fish and meat to live. And I guess there's nothing wrong with killing for sport. It's wrong for me, that's all."

"Then don't do it," Toro said simply. "For a submariner, though, that's pretty weird. Why didn't you get into the medics or something if you've got qualms about hurting anything?"

Keith tried to trace his feelings back. "When that submarine pulled me out of the water, all I wanted to do was to get back at the Japs. But the main thing now is to get it over with. Besides, if everybody was asking to be a corpsman or a chaplain's clerk, we'd lose the war. It's got to be done, and it's my job as much as yours."

The waves crashed upon the sand like assault troops, drawing back with a hissing sound. In the northeast, clouds were piling up against the stars, backlighted with distant heat lightning.

"With me, it's like hunting," Toro said thoughtfully. "You track that *maru* until you've got him cornered, then you put a fish into him."

Keith took a handful of sand and let it trickle from his fist. "Maybe I've got too much imagination. I know we've got to kill or be killed. But after we sink a ship I always remember the *Bataan Trader*—the men in the water with their skin burned black, the ones being cremated in the hold and cooked in live steam. Friends or enemies, when I hear them in the phones, screaming, it makes me sick."

Toro was fascinated. "You mean you can really hear 'em?"

"Sure! Just like an underwater telephone."

Toro pondered, realizing the problem was genuine and wanting to find an answer to it. "You never hunted, I guess."

Keith gave a sour smile. "Not according to my father. I could punch the bull's-eye out of a target, but I couldn't hit anything living. Finally he got suspicious that I was missing on purpose. After that, hunting turned into more of a debate than a sport, and I wound up on the same team with the rabbits."

"What was he trying to prove?" Toro asked curiously.

Keith clenched his hands in the coarse sand. He had never talked to anyone before about his relations with his father. Now he had come to the part which still humiliated and stung. He was not sure whether he knew this big man well enough to tell him; whether he would ever know anyone that well. But something told him it was time to try to get it out.

"He wasn't trying to prove anything," he said. "He was trying to get me to prove something to him."

"What was that?"

"Well—the last time we went hunting, I missed a bunch of quail with a twelve-gauge. I don't think I could have missed them with a flyswatter. I never saw him so mad. He yanked the gun away from me, and then he slapped me. And he said—" He faltered a moment, and then went on: "He said, 'Damn you! Why don't I just sell this thing and buy you a girl's dress and a hair ribbon?' "

Toro looked surprised. But he did not look away in embarrassment, and Keith felt reassured.

"He wanted me to prove to him that I was—wasn't a mama's boy," he said. "Because to him, you couldn't be manly without wanting to kill things. He was a soldier, and that was the way he thought."

Toro nodded, but did not comment.

"He was doing the best he could," Keith said defensively.

"I'm not arguing with you," Toro grunted.

"You see, my mother died when I was a kid. He wasn't geared for being a father-mother combination. After that last hunt, he put me in boarding school. It was better all around."

"Where's your old man now? Being a general somewhere?"

"He's dead. He was on Corregidor."

"I hope he was doin' his manly best."

"That's for sure. All the times we tangled, I never doubted one thing: he was all man."

"You know something, kid? That goes for you, too."

Keith peered at him. "Toro, if you knew how close I was to cracking up when we took that aerial bomb—" he said earnestly.

Toro laughed. "You weren't alone, boy. Ratkowski got sick, and I didn't hear anybody asking for seconds in the messhall. It's just rough, that's all. You sink your teeth in and do your damn' job, and that's what they call submarining.

"Let's hit the sack. I'd like to get out tomorrow before the wind comes up."

They trudged back to the shack on the beach. A feeling of tightness in the back of Keith's neck was gone; he had not been aware of it until suddenly he knew it was there no longer.

He read the letter on the train back to Brisbane.

"I won't pretend at this late hour that I understand you," Colonel Stocker had written. "But that's a fault in me, not in you. People aren't all the same, fortunately. Yet a father somehow likes to see his own reflection when he looks at his son. And what I saw was the reflection of your mother. You have more of her characteristics than of mine. And why shouldn't you have? She was as strong as she was gentle. The thing I've been so slow in realizing is that you're just as much of a fighter as I am, only we don't fight about the same things."

Then there was a gap in the letter, and a new dateline.

"You'll probably have to get into this war, and if you do, you'll find your slot. I haven't the slightest worry about that. Whether you're a stretcher-bearer or a mortarman, you'll be a good one. But whatever you do, do your job like a man, the way my men are doing. *My men*—the proudest words I ever wrote, except for two others: *My son.*"

Keith placed the letter in his pocket and looked out at the dusty countryside. He settled down in the wicker-backed seat and closed his eyes. *"Only we don't fight about the same things."*

It was strange how someone who didn't really understand you could help you to understand yourself.

28

The captain made his usual briefing talk over the communication system a few hours out.

"We're going on station off the Palaus again, and try to make life miserable for the Japanese navy. Our ground forces are beginning to move up through the Solomons. With the Palaus neutralized as a supply base, the campaign will really get into high gear. So we're carrying the ball, and we're going to run off some yardage."

"What about that Jap torpedo we brought home?" the chief asked him, later. "Was it worth all our trouble?"

"I meant to tell you about that," Casey replied. "The thing was full of rice."

"Rice!"

"Plain, ordinary rice. Get the significance?"

"No, sir."

"It means the Japanese are starving on Guadalcanal. They haven't gotten a supply ship through in a couple of weeks. Now they're trying to land supplies by torpedo! Our ground forces can really begin to push."

Mako's famous rice torpedo was an accurate battle barometer. Within a short time, United States forces had secured the entire island and made landings on other islands. The high-water mark of the Pacific war had been reached; now the tide was running north toward Japan itself.

On her third war patrol, *Mako* and her crew hit their stride.

A hundred miles from the Palaus, a big convoy of nine vessels escorted by three destroyers steamed boldly over the horizon. After Casey charted his attack plan, the sub lay in wait until the first ships came on the firing bearing. Then she let the fish go. A gasoline tanker exploded with a tremendous flash and the destroyers began to rush back and forth like hornets.

Mako went deep and the convoy passed, zigging desperately. After the ships were out of sight, the submarine came to periscope depth and picked up their trail again. She picked off three more before two of the warships forced her to resort to deep submergence. The depth charging was long and brutal. Battered, she rose after two hours and gave chase, but the convoy was out of range.

Her diesels growling resentfully, the boat slogged through the hot equatorial currents toward New

Guinea. Sonar picked up the throb of powerful engines, and the sub got ready for a scrap. Outer tube doors opened, she waited to meet the unseen ships. The superstructure of a destroyer came up over the horizon; then the enormous silhouette of a carrier formed on the water. Another destroyer hove into view. The men who got sick during depth chargings were already looking green; the smokers were chain-smoking.

"Look at those ugly brutes!" Casey said. The ship's main circuit was turned on so that his voice, as if accidentally, carried to all compartments. "Parading around like they owned the whole Pacific. Mister Ratkowski, look at that carrier! Does he look familiar?"

The exec took the 'scope. "Not to me, sir. Old one, I think."

"That's the *Soryu!* The carrier that wrecked *Yorktown* at Coral Sea!"

"The *Soryu!*" The exec turned to the phone talker. "Pass the word that we're making an approach on the carrier that sank the old *York!*"

Excitement flared up like paper. The strong juices of anger flowed. Twisting the sound crank back and forth, Keith counted screw beats on the carrier. The attack team huddled like a bone-crushing backfield.

"The book says he's thin-skinned at the stern, Captain!"

"Thanks, Yeo. I think we'll knock out his steering gear, take on the DD's, and then finish him up if he's still afloat."

Casey planned meticulously, matching radar, sonar, and optical bearings. The ten men in the conning tower functioned quietly, a muttered word serving for a sentence, a gesture replacing a word.

The submarine slipped aside as the convoy passed. The carrier was enormous, a great, gray billboard sliding across the sea. Arrogantly, her escort of small boys charged back and forth. One of them suddenly came bearing down squarely upon the submarine, which dove to three hundred feet. The destroyers were not pinging, and their passive sonar did not pick her up. As the heavy screws passed overhead, Casey ordered: "Come to sixty-five feet."

Now he was looking squarely at the stern of the *Soryu*. His manner quickened. "Range—mark!"

"One one double oh!"

"Set depth twenty feet. Make ready the bow tubes. Match gyros forward."

"Torpedo run one five double oh yards. Shoot anytime," Ramage said eagerly.

"Fire *One!* Fire *Two!* Fire *Three!* Fire *Four!* Switching targets."

Before the attack plan on the first destroyer was complete, the fish began to explode. One after the other three torpex warheads crashed magnificently against the carrier's stern. Keith reported the sound of the huge screws stopping immediately. The big ship lay dead in the water. At once the destroyer was turning; but the captain had predicted correctly in which direction he would swing.

"Fire *Four!* Fire *Five!* Take her deep! Rig for depth charge. Rig for silent running."

Submerging at a steep angle, they heard one of the torpedoes crash into the destroyer, then the familiar breaking-up and exploding noises. Keith heard it all—the ripping of metal which meant the slashing open of men's flesh; the blazing explosions, with their postscript of seared flesh—yet it did not touch him. He held his mind rigidly to his job, like an ambulance surgeon seeing the mangled body and thinking calmly of what must be done first.

The second destroyer came after them. They lay silent at three hundred feet. A few depth charges came swirling down through the black water. Ventilation and pipe lines whipped with the thrumming vibration of guitar strings. *Mako* lay passive under the barrage. Then the destroyer rushed back to aid the wounded carrier.

Casey waited until dark; at 2200, he ordered the boat up. "Stand by forward. Stand by aft."

The men were limp with heat and fear, but they functioned. They were a first-string team, and they knew it. Leaking from a dozen wounds, *Mako* surfaced. Fires were blazing on the *Soryu* and the carrier had settled by the stern. Casey spoke quietly until he came to the command of execution. Then he bawled the words that justified the submarine's whole existence:

"*Fire! Fire!*"

The remaining torpedoes forward leaped away. The boat pivoted to present her stern tubes. The first fish began detonating against the carrier's hull as two more leaped across the water. Then she ran at emergency speed, diving and burning up the batteries while they scrambled from the area.

"Captain, I was just thinking," Mister Ratkowski said abruptly. "Seems to me *Soryu* was sunk at Midway. Am I mistaken?"

"You're absolutely right," the skipper said cheerfully. "And *Soryu* didn't actually sink *Yorktown*— he just gave her an awful drubbing. I thought it would be more fun, though, if we made a personal thing out of the attack. I mean, as long as we had to do it anyway."

That was what Chief Jolley had meant, Keith realized, when he said that the Old Man was a hell of a skipper.

29

A rumor swept the boat that *Mako* was slated for a complete refit at Mare Island, San Francisco, after her next patrol. No one really believed it. Yet combat-weary men needed something comforting to believe in, and *Mako*'s men could scarcely afford not to believe it. Everything they needed and dreamed of was wrapped up in that word: *Refit!*

Thirty days' liberty! Stateside food, towns, and girls! Thirty days without a hand shaking you every few hours and a voice growling, "Hit the deck, sailor! You're on watch."

The Chief of the Boat listened cynically to the men's eager discussions of how they would spend their time. At last he said gruffly,

"Watch out, swabbies. Trouble comin'."

"Why?" Keith asked him. He had begun to rely on the old submariner's instinct for what came next.

"I never saw it to fail. Start a featherhead rumor like this and there's grief within twenty-four hours."

"Aw, that's just superstition," Keith grinned.

197

"Think so? Don't let me spoil your fun, then."

The fourth patrol was a hair-raising foray into the Yellow Sea—that busy little wading pond between China and Korea whose water was so shallow that nowhere could an injured sub find deep water to hide in. Almost the first to visit it, *Mako* crept into this murky birdbath and began riotously sinking sampans, barges laden with railroad cars, and big steamers smoking across to Manchuria. But almost immediately, the trouble Chief Jolley had predicted closed upon them.

Fast patrol boats rushed in to harry her with hit-and-run attacks. Dive bombers swept in from Korea. Destroyers charged into the area to clear the Yellow Sea of this unheard-of despoiler of Japan's back-yard shipping. For three days *Mako* was kept pinned down almost constantly. Every time she surfaced, screw sounds would come churning back and she would be driven under again, her battery only half-charged, the air in her compressed air flasks ebbing.

The skipper was haggard with strain. Tempers began to snap. Keith got into foolish arguments with men who hinted that it was partly the sonarman's fault if all he could hear was bad news.

Despite all this grief, the Mare Island rumor flourished. Now it was sixty days' leave and an advance in rate all around! A week at the Royal Hawaiian Hotel in Honolulu on the way back to duty! The Chief of the Boat had nothing to say about all this until the day they sneaked out of the Yellow Sea and headed for the barn. Then he walked into the crew's mess at evening chow with a paper in his hand and a bitter grin on his face.

"Mare Island, huh? Listen to this: 'U.S.S. *Mako* will proceed at once to Midway Island for refit.'"

"Midway!" groaned Hartman. "The worst liberty port in the Pacific. Gooney birds, fly-boys, and sand. Tell us you're kiddin', Chief!"

"Kiddin' with tears in my eyes!" roared Jolley, ripping the paper to scraps and hurling it to the deck before he stomped out.

Mako was only two days en route when things began to go wrong. The men slept poorly after the long days of silent running. Prolonged deep submergence, oxygen starvation, and stunning depth-charge bombardments had left their nerves raw. Disappointment over getting no leave had swept them deep into gloom.

The mathematics of trimming ballast seemed to have become too much for Lieutenant Bratton; the boat always had a down angle or an up angle. Mister Ratkowski found mysterious difficulties in working out the boat's position. Pharmacist's Mate Mettick was kept busy doctoring men with ailments they would have scorned to mention earlier in the patrol.

Captain Casey studied his crew with anxious frowns. Suddenly course was changed. The submarine set course for New Guinea. In a jungle harbor they tied up in the nest of subs alongside a sub tender. The ship was a floating city; a thousand feet long, she housed a bakery, hospital, machine shop, and print shop, and ton upon ton of supplies. When she went to sea, she was guarded by six submarines, four destroyers, and a cruiser. Artisans swarmed through and over *Mako,* patching up her minor wounds while eight of the crew went to sick bay. Replacements for these men came aboard, and one night the sub slipped from the harbor and drove on toward Midway. The men were still depressed.

It was an Italian boy named Vito Rotunno, one of the replacements, who made Casey's Corsairs aware that they were suffering something even more serious than combat fatigue.

Rotunno was a slender youth of twenty. He was brash and boastful, with a moustache which was new and silken, and brows much heavier than the moustache. His upper lip, thicker than the lower, overhung it in an unattractive way. His accent made one think of acres of slum buildings and overflowing trash cans. He had a crooked grin and an absolute conviction that any scuttlebutt session he intruded on was the better for his presence.

From the first, no one liked him. For that matter, the whole catch of replacements was a sorry bunch of sailors.

One day when Keith and some others were having pie before going on watch, Rotunno brought his coffee and pie over and joined them. "Hey, howda you guys stand this old boiler?"

"What's the matter, Rotunno? Is the perfume dispenser in the gentlemen's room empty again?" Rubio sneered.

Rotunno grinned. "Fa Pete's sake," he said, "the air conditioning don't work in half the lousy boat! Why don't you send a letter through channels? You got a right, aincha?"

They ignored him and went back to their low-toned discussion of whether they would go to a new boat after leave, or whether *Mako* would be back in service by then.

"Write the letter tonight," Rotunno persisted. "Git Yeo to write it, he knows the form. Give it to the exec inna morning and—"

"Oh, is that how it's done?" Keith jeered. "How about it, men, we've got a sea lawyer aboard now!"

"Yeah, and listen, put something in about the chow. I heard submarine chow was good, but this slop—"

Coldly, they stared at him. Soper hadn't felt right lately, and his cooking had suffered.

"Ain't there something you ought to be doing?" asked Hartman.

Rotunno, though insensitive, finally realized he was not welcome. For the first time, he showed signs of resentment. His liquid brown eyes narrowed sullenly and he sucked a tooth. "Lookit! they got a club," he said. "The Old Timers' Club, how 'bout it?"

He got up and moved to the next of the long tables.

"Something we got to figure out," said Rubio quietly, "is who's going to write Wilson's wife and tell her he's sick."

Wilson had been detached in New Guinea. They had had to carry him from the sub onto the tender by stretcher. Mettick's diagnosis was that he was seriously ill with a tropical fever.

"A chaplain'll write her," someone said.

"Yeah, but a letter from his buddies would mean a lot to her. You know—make his old lady think he's a war hero and all that?"

Rotunno twisted to flash his cocky grin at them. "Waddya know! We got war heroes on this trainin' ship, now!"

Hartman stood up, bracing to the slow roll of the boat. "If you don't butt out, Rotunno, somebody's gonna get killed."

Rotunno slipped from his seat, lithe and quick. He stared into Hartman's face for a moment and then, without changing expression, hit him on the jaw. Hartman bellowed. Unhurt, he seized Rotunno by the front of his shirt and struck him open-handed, first on one side of his head, then on the other. When the Italian boy struggled, he jammed him against the pipes lining a bulkhead and held him there while he slapped him viciously. He outweighed Rotunno by seventy-five pounds and stood five inches taller. He was white with anger. His mates sat pounding the table, yelling at him to kill Rotunno.

"*Belay that!*" someone roared.

Hartman dropped him. Turning, he saw Captain Casey standing in the compartment, looking sleepy and rumpled, but sallow with anger. "What's the matter, Hartman, did you run out of girls to fight?" Casey snarled.

Hartman walked toward him gesturing. "He made fun of Wilson, Cap'm! Ask anybody."

Every man in the compartment had something to yell, substantiating Hartman's story. As he listened, Casey's face lost its anger. A sad weariness filled his eyes. They all saw it, and one by one stopped shouting. In silence Rotunno rubbed his hands together, bewildered.

"I think maybe we're all a little overwrought," Casey said gravely. "You're due on watch, now. Let's not have a repetition of this. That's an order."

Keith was ashamed of his part in it. Hartman grumbled: "I'd apologize to the slob, but I hate him too much. He shouldn'ta butted in like that."

"All those new guys are buttinskys," Keith agreed.

Until the Submarine Force order broke on them, they did not realize that *any* new man would have been regarded as a buttinsky. As Rotunno had said, they were a club. They were *Mako's* men. They were Casey's Corsairs. Newcomers need not apply.

The order directed: ". . . All submarine commanders will make up transfer lists at the conclusion of any patrol regarded as exceptionally hazardous. One-half the personnel will immediately be made available for reassignment, the remainder continuing as part of the ship's complement. . . ."

In swabbie language it meant that *Mako's* crew was to be broken up, for the good of the Service.

Only one good thing came of the Yellow Sea patrol. After two days at Midway, it was decided that *Mako* was in need of a more complete refit than the island's facilities offered. She was ordered back to the States at that mythical speed only a tired sailor could appreciate:

"All ahead Mare Island! San Francisco, here we come."

Keith spent a month with his aunt and uncle in Los Angeles. He went to moving pictures, swam at the YMCA, read books and magazines, and ate. But he never relaxed during the entire month. A small motor inside him would not shut down. Reading a book, he would find his mind wandering. There was a guilty sensation within him that he should be doing something else—relieving Yeo at the helm; standing a sonar watch.

One day word came that he was to report back to U.S.S. *Mako* at the end of his leave, rather than to a new boat.

When his leave ended, he took a bus back to San Francisco. He found the *Mako* smelling of fresh paint, with new dials on the sonar stack and an improved radar head. The new torpedoes shining in their racks were said to be the most effective yet.

But the men going back to sea were the same. They were efficient and sharp, frugal of words and motions. They were businessmen, and their business was killing. Not a man aboard would have bet money they would ever come back.

Chief Jolley was still awake, reading a training manual in the chiefs' quarters, when Keith glanced in. Jolley had a salute and a grin for him.

"Got a new bunk for you, kiddo. You're on the bottom, across from Rubio. Cooler."

"Oh—thanks." Keith frowned. "Wait a minute, that's— Oh, yeah. I forgot Wilson's gone."

"You can move back to the crew's quarters, if you want. Better air conditioning there, but you'd be in with a lot of green stuff just out of New London. One of them asked me if we'd ever killed any Japs!"

"I hope you told him we just take pictures of Japanese ship launchings."

Jolley chuckled and fanned himself with the training manual. "Well, we lost a few buddies on the

Great Shake-up, boy. I hope the lousy Navy knows what it's doing."

"Anybody gone from my end of the boat?"

"Couple of jokers. I've had my little list for a long time, and I just added to it. We lost all our cigar smokers, except Mister Ratkowski. I hate a cigar. And a certain motor mach named Rainey hadn't taken a bath in so long he had barnacles on his elbows, so I put him up for adoption. Becket—he's gone. He always was a lousy ping jockey. Hartman stays. And that Mexican kid, Rubio, if he ever gets back from leave. I guess we'll survive."

"Sometimes I wonder, Chief," Keith said despondently. "It goes against all the laws of physics to send a steel bubble like this down three hundred feet, slam it around with explosives, and expect it to come up. Sooner or later, the pigboats always run out of luck."

He knew he was right. But he wanted the chief to tell him he was wrong.

"Not all of them. Just some. And if you keep busy, you'll forget the odds. For instance, this here Chief Torpedoman is preparing himself for officer's school." He waved the training manual.

Keith felt a sudden shock. "You're kidding, Chief! You're not leaving the boat?"

Jolley dropped the training manual and linked his fingers under his head. "I wouldn't take a commission if they handed it to me. I got all the privileges and none of the responsibility. At least if I get chewed out for something, it's by one of my own officers, not some admiral on Noumea. But I'm improving myself just the same, even if I don't want the job. Nothing to stop you from studying to be a first, or something."

"No use, Chief. I'm not mechanical enough to get far in this man's Navy. I'm all thumbs and weak on math."

"What about when you get out? What are you going to do for a living?"

"I'd like to study oceanography. Something connected with the sea. Be a marine biologist or technician, maybe. I never want to leave the sea."

"Then pick up some books before we put out and start studying."

"I'll do that," said Keith. "Now I've got to unpack, Chief. See you around."

Jolley's raised finger held him. "Hold it! I'll tell you something special we've got working for us, swabbie. We've got a helluva skipper."

"I know."

"You don't know nothin'!" the chief rapped. "Captain Casey works out more problems in his head during an attack than a math major does in two semesters of calculus. The stuff most skippers have to hand to the X.O. are duck soup for him. If we get back, that's what'll bring us home. That and the J-factor."

"What's the J-factor?"

The chief smiled. "Some people call it luck. I think it's more than that—it's the man upstairs. That's why we call it the J-factor. When we need more help than the captain can give us, that's where it will come from."

30

At Pearl Harbor, more replacements came aboard to bring the boat up to strength. Then *Mako* headed for the sub tender in New Guinea, where they topped off their fuel and restocked supplies used en route. A team of Army Pioneers and demolition men came aboard with metal crates labeled:

Danger! High Explosives!

The submarine rigged for dive and ran for the sea again. The demolition men would be put ashore in the Philippines to dynamite a certain strategic railroad curve above the ocean. After they were picked up, the submarine would cruise to Japanese waters to investigate what the captain said was the wildest rumor yet.

"A seventy-thousand-ton carrier in a harbor southeast of Tokyo! Hell, a flattop that big would have to be three times the size of the *Oklahoma!* Personally, I don't believe it, but intelligence says a carrier's being completed in Funabushi Harbor. We're supposed to take pictures of it if it's still on the ways, or bounce some torpedoes off it if it's in the water."

"Don't know about this going into enemy harbors stuff, Captain," said Scobie, at the helm. "Maybe we better turn the assignment over to the Coast Guard, huh?"

"There's nothing to it, Scobie. We just wait till they open the sub nets and sneak in behind one of their own ships."

"It sounds like fun, sir. How do we get out again?"

"Oh, we don't have to come out," Casey chuckled. "We just have to go in."

Off a feverish jungle coast the boat surfaced and nosed along searching for landmarks. The demolition men assembled in the forward torpedo room, grotesquely streaked with camouflage paint and wearing jungle dress. Each was armed with a Thompson submachine gun, a knife, and a pack containing explosives. They were very young, except for the lieutenant in charge, a hard-jawed man of forty with clipped gray brows. They studied maps while an inflatable boat was being readied.

The captain came forward and slapped the lieutenant on the back. "This is your bus stop, Lieutenant. Did you all wind your watches?"

"Yessir, and I put out the cat. At exactly 0200 tomorrow, we'll meet you here. If there's a change, we'll radio."

"Right. Good luck."

He shook hands with each of them and they climbed through the escape trunk and rowed into the darkness.

The following night the submarine returned. Keith had the port lookout forward. While they waited, a flash of light illuminated the jungle and faded quickly, followed by a remote thud of dynamite. A radio signal was received which meant: "Mission accomplished."

On the submarine, the crew was elated. But a half-hour later sudden gunfire crackled on the beach. Prolonged ripples of automatic weapons fire carried across the water. The gunfire continued until long after the Army men were due to rendezvous with the sub. With everything shut down, the bridge watch listened for the sound of oars. A depressing silence shrouded the boat. Keith strained to see the beach. A faint redness was beginning to stain the sky beyond the jungle-clothed mountains. He swept the glasses back and forth, alert for aircraft. Then he heard Mister Ratkowski mutter:

"Getting light, Captain."

"I know. God, I hate to abandon those kids here! They can't all be dead. Some of them may be rowing out right now."

"The map shows an enemy airfield ten miles north of us, Captain."

"I know, I know!" The skipper's voice crackled with impatience.

Another half-hour passed. Keith's eyes burned from long peering through the binoculars. Specks floated before them. He squeezed them close and reopened them, but the specks remained, sliding down in the way such specks usually did, and standing out clearly now against the deep, greenish-black of the foothills. He frowned and started to adjust the glasses. Then he knew they were planes, and he screamed:

"Aircraft bearing three zero zero!"

The first plane was making its bombing run. It slanted in with pale bursts of flame glowing around its nose gun. Through the conning tower hatch spilled the bridge watch. Keith heard the guns faintly over the diving alarm, and saw streaks of lead dance across the bullnose and begin to chop their way down the deck slats toward the bridge. Something dropped from the plane's belly, skipped twice toward the sub, and sank. An instant later it exploded with a peach-colored flash.

A plume of spray fanned up. The plane flashed over the submarine with its guns raking the decks and bridge. Keith could see the red Rising Sun on the wings. Bullets smacked and whined around the bridge and the periscope shears. *Mako* rocked in the wave from the bomb. Only the captain and Keith were still topside. As Keith prepared to drop to the bridge, he saw Casey fall heavily. Keith jumped down beside him, alarmed. When the captain did not rise, he knelt quickly beside him. "Captain!" Suddenly he felt warm blood on his hands, and saw the wounds in Captain Casey's head and throat. He looked toward the conning tower hatch, stunned. Mister Ratkowski was watching, his face blank. Then his expression hardened and he gestured Keith inside.

"Clear the bridge. We're diving."

"Sir, he's wounded!"

"He's dead, Stocker. Leave him and get inside."

Leave him! Leave the only man who could handle the ship? With his hands clenched together under the captain's chest, Keith started lifting him. White water foamed across the foredeck as *Mako* went into her dive; water exploded against the coaming and drenched them. The captain's head hung loosely, rolling as Keith struggled, sobbing. He looked up at the exec.

"Bear a hand!" he pleaded. "I can almost do it."

"Stocker, *he's dead!* He's shot through the throat! If you want to stay with him, all right. But I'm closing the hatch!"

Keith looked at the captain, wanting to ask him to help. There was the drone of an airplane above. Belowdecks the raucous *aah-ooo-ga!* of the diving alarm continued frantically. The skipper did not move. His eyes were closed and the steady scarlet spurts of blood from his throat had ceased. Keith let him down on the deck and ducked through the hatch, his shoes skidding on the rungs. Hartman reached up, closed the hatch and dogged it tight.

At full power, fighting for her life, the sub chewed green water at a sharp down angle. Keith grabbed a big valve and hung on as the dive angle increased. He heard Ratkowski giving orders as calmly as though it were a training dive. *He's not worth Casey's little finger!* he thought furiously. *He's all spit and polish and bluff.*

"All ahead emergency! Two hundred feet. Rig for depth charge. Planesmen, watch your angles."

Keith looked at the depth gauge. Fifty feet. The bridge was under and now the skipper was gone. He was staring at Mister Ratkowski when the exec turned his head and caught the bitterness in his face.

"Stocker, relieve the sound man."

Keith wiped his hands. Feeling their stickiness, he glanced down and saw blood on them. "I'd like to wash off the blood first, sir," he said.

"I said relieve the sound man!" The exec seized him by the shoulders and shoved him across the compartment. The sonarman pulled off the phones and relinquished the console. Keith sat down and automatically reached for the crank. When he heard water splash, he pulled off the phones and yelled,

"Aerial bomb at zero two five!"

A detonation rocked the boat. Cork insulation flew; deckplates and gratings clattered. Then the boat was under the surface and diving smoothly. A few minutes later, the exec said:

"Secure from depth charge. Come right ten degrees."

In the silence, Lieutenant Bratton came up from the diving station. "Dammit," he complained to the executive officer, "we've got our hands full now, haven't we?"

"What a helluva way to go!" someone said. But the exec said wearily:

"Never begrudge a submariner a quick death. It's the least he's entitled to."

31

The conning tower was silent. Up and down the boat, the crew stood somberly at their stations. Mister Ratkowski walked the periscope around, searching the hot gray sea as though he still prayed to see the captain waving for help. But that was two hours ago. He had radioed ComSubPac word of the catastrophe and asked for instructions.

Instructions were curt: "Assume duties as commanding officer and carry on with patrol."

Lieutenant Bratton, the engineer officer who had acted as diving officer, became executive officer. All posts were now filled except one. That was the one no one could ever fill, Keith thought. Relieved at the end of his watch, he went down to the messhall. He carried a cup of coffee and a sandwich to the table, but the chicken sandwich tasted like plaster and the sight of Soper standing with a long face in the galley was enough to take anyone's appetite.

Word had gotten around that Keith was the last man to see the captain alive. Everyone waited for him to tell about it, but no one wanted to ask. Then Chief Jolley came through the airlock from the engine room and started forward. Seeing Keith, he sat down across from him. Everyone in the compartment was listening. Jolley touched Keith's coffee cup.

"Aren't you drinking this?"

Keith shook his head. Jolley put it down at a gulp. He thumped the cup on the table, and sighed. "Well, the J-factor let him down," he said. "I hear you were with him?"

"Yes."

"How'd it happen?"

"Bullet through the throat."

Jolley nodded. "Quick and easy."

"Not for us," said Keith.

"No. Not for us. He was a real fightin' skipper, kiddo. He had more math in his head than most public libraries have on their shelves, and more scrap in his heart than any ten men I ever knew. Hartman, howsabout gettin' me some more java?"

Toro was about to carry the empty cup to the galley when Soper came hurrying out in his dishtowel apron with a fresh cup. Jolley sweetened the coffee with four spoonfuls of sugar, taking his time, as though he enjoyed making the men wait.

"Yes, sir, he was a helluva skipper," he pronounced. "But you know one reason why he was good?"

They waited. When a man clinked a spoon against his cup, everyone scowled at him for making such a clatter.

"He was tops because he had the best executive officer in the Pacific. He didn't have to worry about the boat being taken care of, or true and relative bearings getting fouled up on the Is-Was. When Casey said 'frog,' Mister Ratkowski saw to it everybody jumped. He's still seeing to it, and you swabbies better jump to battle stations when you hear that gong!"

For the next few days *Mako* plowed through rough seas, her exhausts barking as the bow smashed through the black water and the swells slid back and crashed against the base of the conning tower, drenching everyone on the bridge. They went on station in the cold waters off Japan.

The harbor which was their destination was a hundred and fifty miles down the coast from Tokyo. The whole area was hazardous, the water roiled by dozens of fast patrol boats and larger men-of-war on guard against just such menaces as *Mako*. Captain Ratkowski followed the shoreline closely, painstakingly studying charts and landmarks. He kept the sonar speaker turned on for long periods. His manner of command was less flexible than that of Captain Casey. He delegated nothing he could handle himself, and his orders were explicit. All this care made the crew uneasy.

Was he overanxious? Afraid he couldn't handle the boat? He reminded Keith depressingly of a diver shivering on a high platform, rehearsing his dive in his mind until he was afraid to leave the mat.

One night Keith had a lookout watch. A cold rain was falling, the ship rolling slowly in a stormy sea. The ocean buckled and broke before the boat as it thrust southeast. From time to time prolonged ripples of lightning would illuminate a background of low mountains. Through the talk-back circuit the sonarman in the conning tower kept reporting ship activity. The captain showed the greatest interest in these reports. He kept scanning the coastline through his glasses, muttering at the rain which spattered them. Suddenly he said,

"Stand by to dive!"

The boat dived to periscope depth and Keith relieved the sonarman. After consulting with his officers, the skipper said,

"Pass the word that we are outside Funabushi Harbor. We'll wait here till they open the nets to let a ship in and try to get inside before they close them. We'll have a partial sonar blackout working for us. The smoking lamp is lit."

Everyone silently prayed, *Don't let those nets open, God! If we can't get in, they can't blame us.*

Or if we get in, let that ship of theirs be on the ways so we won't have to shoot at it. Then maybe we can get out again.

After exactly five minutes the captain ordered cigarettes extinguished. No one knew how long the submarine would be submerged, nor when the air conditioning would have to be secured. As he studied charts and tide tables, the captain chewed a pencil. Mister Bratton worked up an enlarged chart of the harbor on a sheet of tracing paper. Keith stole a glance at it. The harbor was shaped like a dog's leg, the wide portion open to the sea, the leg itself kinking to the right at the midpoint.

Somewhere in that harbor, if their information was correct, was the biggest ship ever built. All they had to do was to sink it—shove a torpedo through twenty inches of steel plate and hit a vital spot. And then, although this was not part of their orders, get out.

32

Slowly the boat cruised at one-third speed back and forth outside the harbor, waiting. The captain kept up a little headway to make the job of trimming ballast easier for the diving officer. Toward dawn a big freighter steamed up from the south. In the leaden rain, signals flashed from the bridge to the net tenders, two small ships with heavy booms aft for rolling back the nets. Smoke poured from their stacks as they labored away from each other, dragging open the heavy submarine nets which hung from large steel balls floating in the water. The freighter steamed through the opening into the harbor.

Captain Ratkowski snapped up the periscope handles. "Down 'scope! All ahead full. Steady as you go."

Mako stole silently along in the freighter's wake. Many of the crew had removed their shoes in their anxiety to observe silence. They did their jobs soberly and with only the necessary words. Keith stolidly watched the dials, turned the knobs, and tried to make himself believe it was merely a normal submarine operation. But every nerve in his body, every cell of his brain, was oversensitized. He remembered a boxing match in which he had been punched all over the ring for three rounds; sitting on the stool waiting for the last round, he had wondered whether he could go out. It was the raw, mistreated flesh that had hurt worst.

Scobie had expressed the feeling after a surface battle in which he had been scared witless. "Man, my nerves was squirmin' just like sandpapered snakes!"

"Sound, keep the bearings coming," Ratkowski said tersely. "We'll trail him a while before we run up the 'scope."

Rules of the road would keep other craft from crossing too close ahead or astern of the freighter. Thus they had some protection even though running blind.

"Nets closing behind us."

Dead silence in the boat. In the conning tower, Lieutenant Ramage stood by with the camera. The captain ran up the 'scope.

"Sun's up. The rain's stopped. The AK is still following the right-hand channel. Down 'scope."

"I'll take a light reading next time you look, Captain," Ramage said, "in case we have to settle for a picture of the ship on the ways."

"Very well."

Keith twisted the sound gear lever back and forth. "Heavy screws bearing zero one five!"

The captain swiveled the periscope around. "Destroyer," he said. "Take a single ping for depth. We'll have to dive."

The ping came back. "Two nine five feet, sir."

"Control, go to two five zero feet."

As they sank, there was a steady *peep-peep-peep!* of a ship pinging around. It passed overhead and went on. "Oh, man!" Scobie moaned, at the steering wheel. Ratkowski ordered the boat back to periscope depth. They had lost their seeing-eye dog now, and must do everything by sound and occasional glimpses through the periscope.

"Okay, we're well down the dogleg. Naval craft docked to the right. On the left, commercial docks. Far end of the harbor, a big installation of some kind. Mister Bratton, are you making a chart as we go?"

"Yes, sir!"

As the skipper stepped back from the periscope, Ramage jumped forward with a light meter in his hand. "Captain, I'll—"

"Later."

"Yessir!"

Keith smiled to himself. It was surprising how military everyone had suddenly become. Probably it was an instinctive submission to the captain's will —seeking safety through trust in a superior being. For a half-hour they crept toward the toe of the sock they had chosen to enter. Sweat streamed from the helmsman as he worked to hold the submarine to the exact compass course. Planesmen watched their bubbles critically. Ratkowski studied a tide table, trying to guess at the current streaming against *Mako*'s hull, which might pull her off course. But most of it had to be done by instinct.

"Stand by for range and bearing. Stand by with the light meter. Up periscope."

The slim tube hummed up out of the periscope well. "Range, fifteen hundred yards. Bearing, three five five."

"We've drifted. Come left ten degrees rudder. Okay, Mister Ramage."

Sweating in his old red tee shirt, Ramage pressed the light meter to the eyepiece and read the available light. "Got it!"

"Down 'scope. Come to one hundred feet."

As the boat leveled off, the captain looked at the chart the exec was sketching. "I've got a problem for you. If an object in the periscope fills so many degrees of the high-power scale at such and such a distance, how long is it?"

"What are the figures, Captain?"

He fed Mister Bratton the figures. The exec said,
"About a thousand feet."

"That's what I got, too."

"What is it?"

"A flattop. The biggest carrier in the world."

Someone in the conning tower dropped a pencil.
Everyone but the captain jumped as though a gun
had been fired.

33

"It looks like we got here just in time," the captain said. He was taking another look through the periscope. "The brute's all duded up with bunting. It was probably launched within the last couple of days. I don't think the flight deck's finished, even."

"Then why was it launched?" asked the executive officer.

"Maybe they're getting nervous about leaving it in one place so long. Probably they're moving it to another harbor—you know, like a soldier heading for a safer foxhole."

Scobie took his eyes off the compass. "Cap'm, how are we going to sink a thing like that?"

"With torpedoes. Plus the well-known factor of luck. There are sailors and workmen crawling all over it," he observed. "What a mess! It looks like a carnival. Maybe we can make that mess work for us, eh?"

"How?" asked Lieutenant Ramage.

"A boat that new might not have watertight bulkheads, efficient damage-control parties, or any sense of teamwork. Three thousand sailors who couldn't be called a crew. If we put a fish well aft, and deep, we may start a fire they can't put out. If they've got their ammo aboard, they'll blow the whole boatyard to pieces when they go up. Pass the word, battle stations torpedo! Don't sound the alarm. Open all outer doors. Range—mark!"

The atmosphere twanged to an unbearable tautness. Keith listened around, screening the many sounds—fishing boats, patrol boats, pumps on nearby ships. The air was soggy with damp heat. The normal two gallons of water which evaporated from a man's body daily simply ran from the pores in streams when the atmosphere could not absorb it. In the conning tower, there was scarcely a sound; only the slight rustle of men tensely doing their jobs.

"Make ready all forward tubes. Set depth twenty-two feet."

"Set!"

"Five-second intervals. Down 'scope."

"Sir!" the executive officer whispered. "This is just a thought, but what if we came about and used our stern tubes? Then we'd be in position to take off fast and use our forward tubes on anything that got in our way!"

Keith thought, *He's right! We'd save a lot of time, and we could fight our way out.* Why hadn't the captain thought of it?

"This is another thought," the captain retorted sharply. "We've got six tubes forward and four aft. Our chance of killing him is fifty per cent better forward. Also, the big danger after we shoot is going to be astern, not ahead. There's a big cruiser under steam at the naval dock. He'll be on our tail fast."

Everyone in the conning tower felt better. The captain was obviously right. But then Hartman asked the question there was no answer for.

"How do we get back through the nets, Captain?"

"I don't know, Quartermaster. I'm offering a five-dollar prize to the first man who comes up with the right answer to that. Whatever happens, we're about to make submarine history."

The boat moved at slow speed into perfect firing range. Keith was thinking of some letters he had put off writing. He was perfectly sure, now, that he was never going to get them written. Never be able to let his aunt and uncle know that he appreciated what they had done for him. Never be able to explain to that fine, suntanned girl at the University who kept writing him what it was like to experience a depth charge. Not many men could predict when they were going to die. But the men on *Mako* could write down their birth and death dates and not miss the latter by twenty-four hours.

"Range—mark!"

"Eleven hundred yards."

"Set!" whispered Lieutenant Ramage.

"Bearing—mark!"

"Three four zero."

Mister Ramage cranked a reading into the portion of the TDC called the "position keeper." In the forward torpedo room certain adjustments would automatically be made in the gyros controlling the courses of the torpedoes.

"Set!"

Moving at steady speed, the boat pushed in closer. In the control room the diving officer stood behind Chief Jolley at the hydraulic manifold. Their private battle was coming. By flooding and venting they had to keep the boat from thrusting her prow into view when those six fish leaped away. The captain held the periscope wire on the stern of the giant ship.

"Final firing bearing and shoot!" It was the captain's first command decision. And it was against the biggest ship ever built.

"Fire One!"

"Fire Two!"

"Fire Three!"

"Fire Four!"

"Fire Five!"

"Fire Six!"

Thirty seconds ticked away while the fish ran out. Then: *WHAM! WHAM! WHAM!* The explosions began to come with measured ferocity through the sub's hull.

"Right in the stern!" shouted the captain. "The flame's crawling up his side. They're running around like ants on a hot stove!"

One after another, all six torpedoes detonated against the carrier. In the phones, the sound was ear-splitting—the crumpling of steel, explosions, then a frying noise like water spilling into hot fat.

"We've breeched him, Captain! He's shipping water!"

"It'll take more than that," the captain reported. "Come to one eight zero and let's give him the stern fish."

Before *Mako* had completed her turn, Keith heard a series of muffled booms as boilers exploded in the flattop. Crackling noises followed like the sharp detonations of exploding firecrackers. Then there was a tremendous blast of high explosives.

"Ammo locker!" the captain yelled. "The whole midships section's ripped open. We got him! All ahead flank! Sound, keep sweeping around."

Keith's skivvy shirt was drenched. His skin itched, and he fought to keep from dropping the soundhead lever and scratching wildly. A powerful throbbing rose in the phones.

"Heavy screws bearing zero two zero!"

"It's the cruiser."

"Fast heavy screws bearing zero four five!"

"Destroyer," the captain said, after taking a quick observation. "Down 'scope. Close outer doors forward, make ready the stern tubes. Start the reload forward."

A bright morning had succeeded the stormy night. Since the periscope feather would be clearly visible, the sub would have to run blind most of the way out. As the boat gained speed, Keith could hear propellers coming closer astern. A ragged pattern of depth-charge booming followed them at a distance.

"Sound, what speed do you give them?"

"Thirty knots on the nearest destroyer, Captain. I can't separate the others."

Captain Ratkowski swore. "Fine! We're doing twelve and it's two miles to the nets. Pass the word to the engine room to get some speed out of those motors. Plot, give me a course to put a couple of fish down his throat at a thousand yards."

He seemed angry rather than anxious, and his vengeful mood affected the whole conning tower. The plotting party worked feverishly in the sodden heat. *Mako* had to slow to one-third speed as the firing bearing began to be reached, in order to increase the chance of a hit. Meantime the destroyer roared in upon them, lobbing shots at the periscope with his five-inchers every time the captain took a look.

"Range, one oh double-oh yards, Captain."

"Shoot!"

The ship bucked as the first fish streaked from

the tube. Poppet valves clattered and the flood of compensating water rushing into the bilges cut off with a deafening shudder. A second fish roared away and they waited. Explosions astern told them that the gunners were firing at the torpedoes. But they were set to run deep. The skipper ordered the periscope up again.

"He's turning away! It's going right into his bows!" They could feel the thunder through the thin steel-plate of the pressure hull, jolting them as the destroyer took the shot. "He's broken off at the bow! All ahead flank! Course one six five. Burn up those batteries!"

Beyond the curtain of noise they raced silently for the harbor mouth. Keith felt sick. He closed his eyes and talked to himself about luck and the J-factor; but even in his imagination he could not picture the nets opening. A quarter-mile from the nets, the captain rang all stop and hit the fathometer key. Three hundred and fifty feet.

"Go to three hundred feet and secure everything."

Keith heard scratchy noises which he supposed were antisub nets dragging on the bottom. Then a throbbing sound began to grow, a sound with power in it that suddenly and unmistakably represented the roar of the oncoming cruiser.

"*Control, get this boat down!*" The captain switched on the sonar speaker and counted beats. "Give him thirty-five knots. Fine! He's got to go through the nets—he hasn't room to stop. There may be more like him along soon. Nobody wants his heavies trapped in a harbor with a submarine. The tin cans are supposed to do for us inside the harbor while the big ones run for the open water."

A moment later Keith reported, "Nets are opening, sir!"

Suddenly there was a soft impact that stopped the submarine's fast descent so abruptly that everyone was thrown to the deck. Gear clattered from lockers. Keith climbed back onto the swing-out stool.

"Oh, man!" Rubio moaned. "And to think the Admiral wanted me to caddy for him at Coronado!"

Nerves bruised too often began to quiver. Lips parted, eyes staring, the men watched the captain.

"Report damage!"

"Conn, F.T.R. No damage."

"Conn, for'd battery. No damage."

The boat had come through it with no obvious damage. "We must be on a mudbank," the skipper decided. "Apparently the fathometer took its depth from a reef. What's the cruiser doing?"

"Directly overhead, Captain. Passing over at one seven zero. One seven five. One seven eight."

The captain ordered all buoyancy tanks blown. But *Mako* was stuck fast. "All back emergency," he said grimly. The electric motors whirred softly. Suddenly she came loose. Immediately she went into a wild climb. Her planes still being reversed, her stern rose above her bow. In the galley, dishes crashed from shelves. Gear banged and clattered. In addition, she was rising too fast to be controlled.

"Vent all main ballast! Vent safety!"

Mako began rocking. The depth gauge needle dropped. She came level, but a moment later it was the bow which was too high. *"Flood negative! Control, bring her up flat! We're going to broach!"*

Despite everything, the submarine burst from the sea into the sunlight, gleaming like a trout. Keith heard the cruiser's screws immediately change in pitch. Then he picked up the sound of the net tenders trying to come about to close the net behind the cruiser.

"Pull the plug! All ahead emergency! Course, one zero zero!"

"Open outer torpedo doors forward! Plot, we're going to give her a couple in the stern. Range—mark! Bearing—"

Muffled thunder shook the sub. A second explosion jarred the conning tower. Scobie bawled, "He's firing on us!" The shell had been a big one, possibly a five-incher. Another shell landed closer. Ratkowski shouted at the diving officer to get her under. They were still trying to square up after broaching, but the boat had her superstructure still above water. As diving officers said, she had "hung up" on her dive.

A deafening screech of steel resounded in the

tower. There was a smell of smoke. Something landed resoundingly on the deck. A man screamed.

"My arm! My arm! Oh, my God!"

Startled, Keith turned. Scobie, who had had the helm, lay on his back on the deck. He was pounding the deck with his uninjured arm. His right arm, nearly severed above the elbow, was hanging by a few white tendons. Astonishingly red, his blood flowed over the green linoleum deck.

Keith became aware of something else. A jagged hole had been ripped through the starboard bulkhead. Something had smashed through the steel wall, tearing pipes and wiring into a tangle. With cold shock, he saw a smoking cylinder with a rounded point lying on the deck. It was a five-inch shell. It had penetrated the conning tower wall but failed to explode. Now it lay on the deck near the forward bulkhead, a few feet from where Scobie was lying. Smoke still curled from it as its fuse burned inside the steel nose.

Captain Ratkowski saw it at the same instant and gave a yell. *"Live shell! Clear the conn!"*

34

As things went on submarines, the first man to leave the conning tower was the man who could not walk—Scobie. Two men handed him down to his mates in the control room. While this took place, the phone talker tried phone circuits until he found one that had not been shorted out. As he repeated the skipper's commands, water began gushing through the hole in the side of the boat. *Mako* was finally submerging. The water covered the deck and spilled down the hatch.

"Isolate the conning tower. Cut off all power. Damage-control party to the control room. Mister Bratton, let's get this thing under water!"

The shell was no longer smoking. Perhaps the heat generated in ripping through the steel hull had caused the smoke. A crewman threw some jackets over the shell to prevent its rolling. The water had already covered the deck and was flooding through the hatch. One after another, the men jumped down the hatch, Hartman going last. He pulled the hatch cover closed and dogged it down.

In the control room there was a feeling of confusion. Sweating electrician's mates were flipping series and banks of switches in the panels before them. Men wearing phones relayed reports up and down the ship. The diving officer ordered, "Blow safety and isolate!" compensating for the weight of the flooded compartment. Scobie lay on the deck, making snoring sounds as he writhed slowly back and forth. Hartman probed for the blood vessels which would stem the bleeding.

"Pharmacist's mate to the control room on the double!"

Mettick arrived and went to work. Wayman, the relief sonarman, was already at the stand-by sonar console in the forward torpedo room. They were at two hundred feet and still descending. The conning tower had been completely isolated from the ship.

"Hold at two-fifty, and make those motors smoke. We've got to get through the nets before they close!"

Lieutenant Bratton stood behind Chief Jolley, a spraddle-legged giant at the hydraulic manifold. He murmured something and Jolley pulled a lever. The captain and Mister Ramage were discussing the shell lying a few feet above their heads.

"If it's H-E," said Ramage, "we've got trouble when it decides to go off."

"But if it's fragmentation, we're all right.—Sound,

what do you hear?" the skipper asked over the phone.

"Nets are still closing but we're going through! The cruiser is dead ahead and still pinging on us."

A moment later he announced that they were outside the nets. The nets had stopped closing now and the destroyers were heading through also.

"Captain, what course?" the helmsman called in alarm, suddenly realizing he did not know what course Scobie had been steering.

"Steady as you go."

So far they had not been seriously hurt, since the conning tower was primarily a carbon copy of the control room. Mettick had tied off the main blood vessels in Scobie's arm, but the gunner's mate was still bleeding profusely. The blood welled thick and red through a pressure bandage. Mettick extracted a stretcher from its stowage and had Scobie carried to the crew's quarters.

The captain ordered the air conditioning turned on. "The smoking lamp is lit."

Men looked at each other. They knew now that he expected the worst. He was trying to freshen the air a little before motors were secured for prolonged silent running; he was giving the men a last opportunity to smoke. Oxygen conservation would soon be too important to permit smoking.

Wayman reported that they were passing under

the cruiser, and a moment later they heard depth charges exploding aft. The cruiser, at least as surprised as *Mako* by the sudden encounter, was not performing well. As they passed under, it turned to go with them. A few seconds later Wayman made the first of the reports which were like a death sentence.

"Fast screws at two six five."

"Go to three five zero feet."

"Repeat?" The diving officer looked around.

"Three hundred and fifty feet."

"Yes, sir."

"Fast screws at zero nine four."

At three hundred and fifty feet, all compartments were asked to report on leakage. Then the captain ordered her down another thirty feet. At last he said, "Secure air conditioning. The smoking lamp is out."

The first depth charges were not close enough to hurt. But they could hear the wrathful destroyers pinging as they charged back and forth—ping-*pingggg!* ping-*pingggg!*—and soon the ashcans were exploding close overhead. Keith was in the messhall when the first near-hit jarred the boat. A clang like someone operating a jackhammer against his head resounded in his skull. The boat's sides buckled and snapped.

"Pull in your necks!" someone gasped. "Here it comes!"

As the detonations slammed the boat, the noise grew unbearable. Lockers were shaken open and contents scattered about. The piping set up its unnerving thrumming, like the deepest bass-fiddle strings imaginable. Keith held onto the table until the rim of it bruised his ribs. Then he tried crouching with his knees bent. A piece of cork insulation fell on his head. The air was filled with dust, paint chips, and bits of glass from shattered light globes. The familiar emergency lights glowed. They could hear light sheet-metal seams and fastenings popping loose.

Soper put on the battle phones. "Water flooding the antenna trunk. Main induction valve leaking."

The barrage died. At once another destroyer started its run. Like a slow-paced string of firecrackers, the explosions ripped athwart the sub. In her torment, *Mako* twisted and writhed. As electrical circuits were shorted out, the electrician's mates worked frantically in the rising heat to restore service.

And in all this hell of noise and damage, Mettick worked quietly over Gunner's Mate Scobie.

35

By midnight they knew the Japanese were going to stay with the job until they finished it. Six warships were taking part in the attack. The constant *Whang! Whang! Whang!* had opened a dozen leaks and broken half the gauges on the boat. The heat stood at 135 degrees. All hands were nearly naked, with rags tied around their foreheads to soak up the perspiration streaming down into their eyes. The bulkheads and overheads were beaded with moisture.

On his bunk in the forward torpedo compartment, Scobie lay waxen and still. Mettick was a good pharmacist's mate, but he was not a doctor. Nor did he have hospital equipment to work with. Loss of blood had drained strength and color from the wounded man, and shock held him in a corpselike stillness.

"What do they expect me to do?" Mettick would complain to anyone who would listen. "I've got no plasma, and I don't know how to administer whole blood. If I did, it wouldn't do any good, because he's in what you call deep shock."

"If you ask me," Jolley said, "you're in deep shock, too. Nobody's blamin' you. Shut up and hang on, 'cause here they come again."

And they came. With their terrible explosives ripping great chasms in the thick water. *Click, BANG! swish.* . . . The water hissed through *Mako*'s superstructure and she rolled in agony. The detonations never ended. The dark lustre of water in the bilges reached the danger point. Water leaked through the safety inboard vent. Men were getting sick; men were fainting. Mettick kept handing out salt pills. The skipper roamed the boat looking things over.

"Captain, what if that shell goes off?"

"It'll break every piece of glass in the conn. Otherwise, probably nothing will happen."

Carbon dioxide absorbent was scattered on the greasy deck to clear the air. A bucket brigade moved the water from one flooded compartment to another to prevent grounding out the motors. Soper made sandwiches. No one ate them.

Rubio dropped onto the bench across from Keith in the messhall. "Rotunno's sick. These new guys are a pain. What'd they think submariners do— chase fish around Pearl Harbor?"

Keith laid his head on his arms and mumbled, "Go start a pool on when the barrage will lift, citizen. I'm sick, too."

In a scared, changed voice, Hector said: "It isn't going to lift, Stock. This time we're going to the bottom."

Keith wearily looked up. "Aw, now, look! You're the one who cheers people up. We'll be out of here before Christmas."

"I'll put ten dollars on Thanksgiving."

Then both men crouched as a salvo of ashcans came raining down, hammering the boat's stern down at a ten-degree angle. When it was over, Hec said bitterly,

"It's not that I wanted to live forever. Just that there was so many things I was going to do."

"You've made your pile, and now they won't let you spend it? I'm cryin', Hec."

Rubio's dark eyes were full of misery. "No, no, Stock, that ain't it. Gambling was just the way of getting money for what I wanted to do."

"What was that?"

"Build a school. Don't repeat that! We might get out yet, and guys won't gamble with you if they think you're giving their money away."

"A school! What for?"

"In my town there's four hundred people and one room for kids to go to school in. Three grades! Just enough education to make a kid wish he didn't have any at all. How about a man with third-grade education trying to support a family, huh? So I was going to build a school and hire a teacher."

Keith smiled. "Rubio Elementary! Hec, I think that's great."

"Every time the money ran out, I was going to come back to the States and play some more poker."

"You're a tough one, all right. But I'll keep your secret. It'd be too bad if it got out that you gambled for anything but personal gain."

Hec grinned and wiped the sweat from his face. "Thanks, Stock. I wouldn't want my reputation ruined so late in the war."

Through the night Scobie's mates shuffled forward to see how he was making it. He rallied briefly and recognized Hartman, once. "Hi, Bull!" he whispered. "Whatcha hear from the mob?" But then he sank again into waxen silence, and they knew he was dying. Mettick strapped him to his bunk to prevent him from being hurled to the deck by the incessant blasts outside the hull. A little after dawn, the pharmacist's mate came to the control room.

"Captain—" he said, and stopped.

"Is he dead?"

"Yessir. Captain, they oughtta be court-martialed for sending a boat out without a real doctor aboard! A doctor coulda—"

"A doctor couldn't have done any more than you. Nothing could have saved him. Get some sleep, fella. You look like the wrath."

Now a rage seized the whole boat, as news of

Scobie's death spread. Fantastic schemes were devised for getting even with the Japs.

"Why couldn't we secure everything, turn her up to a forty-five degree angle, and fire fish at them?"

"What if we jettisoned a few thousand gallons of oil and sent up a recognition flare? The flare would set fire to the oil and they'd have to clear out. Then we'd—"

"Why couldn't we make mines out of five-gallon cans and torpex? They'd plow into them, and—"

Some of these schemes were taken to the captain, who listened gravely. "I'll think it over. Glad you're on your toes, men."

It was after this that he muttered to the exec, "If we don't slip out of the trap pretty soon, we'll have eighty maniacs on our hands."

"You've thought about releasing oil and air to make them think they've killed us?"

"That's my hole card. Point is, we may need that air to breathe before we're through. How much oxygen have we used up?"

"About half."

At 1630, Jolley announced to the men gathered in the crew's mess, "That's it! Twenty-four hours submerged. The next twenty-four should be easy."

Hartman said huskily, "If we get out, it'll be tonight. We can't stay more'n a few more hours, and we can't get away by day."

"Good head, that Hartman," Jolley said sarcastically.

Toro leaped at him, knocking him down with a blow to the jaw. Jolley gave a roar and started up. Soper threw a bucket of water on him and several men piled on each antagonist. After a moment they settled down. No one commented on the fight.

During the early hours of the second night the barrage seemed to ease. The men began to take heart. The captain allowed smoking, but there was so little oxygen in the air that cigarettes would not stay lit. They had now been submerged for twenty-seven hours. Then a hell of concussions broke loose. Damage was reported in the after torpedo room. As the water rose, the compartment had to be isolated. They could not run the pumps to lower the rising water, but compressed air was bled in from the high compression line as the boat began to settle by the stern.

Keith took over the helm watch. A number of men had lost consciousness, and oxygen had to be used to revive them. The main oxygen tanks were nearly empty.

"About that time, Chief," the captain told Jolley. "We'll blow all the air we can spare, and then open one of the fuel tanks."

"Yessir. Which fuel tank?"

The captain pressed his fingers against his eyes, trying to think. "A forward tank."

Mister Bratton was sitting spraddle-legged on the deck, a limp cigarette in his fingers. He looked up as Captain Ratkowski said softly, "Chief, I've got an idea."

"What's that, sir?"

"Scobie."

"What about him?"

"You know as well as I do that a little oil and air won't fool the Japs. But Scobie might."

Drooping heads came up while he explained it to the chief. Mettick looked shocked; he staggered from the compartment to tell others what was going on. Keith was fascinated and slightly repelled.

The idea was to fit the dead man out with a life jacket and Momsen lung and send him up through a torpedo tube after the oil and air trick had been performed.

"They'll think they've breeched us. Scobie'll look like a survivor trying to escape. Naturally, they wouldn't expect anybody to come up alive from this depth."

He breathed some pure oxygen from an 02 line to clear his head. Picking up a phone, he cut into the main circuit. "Now, hear this! They can outstay us, but they can't outfox us. When the diving alarm sounds, I want everybody to pound on the deck with anything that'll make a noise. Secure after ten seconds."

Mettick came back with Soper and three other men. They staggered up to the captain.

"Captain, we think it's the lousiest trick that was ever pulled on a submariner! To—to just push him out like garbage!"

"Belay that!" Ratkowski said.

"He's got a wife and kid. Are you going home and tell them what you did?"

"I'm not going anyplace unless those destroyers take off! I'll give Scobie's wife a medal in his name and tell her nothing about it. And you're going to obey orders, all of you, or I'll have you put in irons. Mister Bratton, take care of things forward and let me know when he's in the torpedo tube. Chief, collect some papers and pillows and cork and anything else that'll float and send it up with him. This has got to look real."

Ten minutes later, the word came back, "Ready forward!"

The skipper pulled the diving alarm. As the raucous horn penetrated the foul air, the submariners howled and beat on the deck with tools and pans. Sound operators a half-mile distant could not possibly fail to hear the racket. If it sounded like breaking-up noises, that was what the captain wanted. As the pounding ceased, Jolley sent compressed air rumbling and hissing through the torpedo tubes. Fuel oil went gurgling into the sea, swirling to the surface to glisten under the searchlights. The depth charges suddenly tapered off. After another ten minutes, the captain said:

"All right, Mister Bratton."

A hiss of air, an oiled whir of machinery. Gunner's Mate Scobie was on his way to glory.

Silence pressed in through the hull. On that thin film of water dividing sea and sky, the warships floated warily at half-speed. Seamen in a barge would examine the dead man and see his escape lung. But would this convince them that *Mako* had been crushed, and a few survivors were trying to make it to the surface? Or would they be made suspicious by Scobie's bandages?

Suddenly Keith turned up the volume control.

Tat-tat-tat-tat-tat! Tat-tat-tat-tat-tat! The diaphragms of the phones rattled to a new sound. He looked up at the captain, who was wiping his face on a towel. "Machine gun!" he whispered.

A few more depth charges rolled down, detonating high above the sub. Elated, the captain whispered: "They're going for it! They've shortened the range to kill anybody floating up."

A moment later:

"Screws turning away at one six three!"

"Screws turning away at two three five!"

"Screws turning away. . . . Screws turning away. . . ."

On the submarine men wept or tried to muffle hysterical laughter. One by one the destroyers quit the area. A single set of propellers was left to stir the water. The captain allowed a trickle of oil and air to rise, as though the sea monster were slowly bleeding to death. At last the final destroyer steamed victoriously back to its hideout.

Leaking from a hundred small wounds, *Mako* crept painfully from the sunless battlefield.

36

On a cold October night, U.S.S. *Mako* plowed past Ballast Point and entered San Diego harbor, battered and brine-stained from her last long patrol. Spray, smashing over the bow before a strong wind, lashed Keith's face and submarine jacket as he stood on the slats of the foredeck. Gazing around the harbor he felt a shiver of excitement. Lights glittered everywhere in the cold, clear air. Street lamps along the waterfront burned yellow; ribbons of red, green, and white light from ships at anchor zigzagged across the choppy water.

The war was over. The lights had come on again.

The great net Japan had flung out across Asia and the rich islands of the Pacific had pulled back empty. A month ago—September, 1945—the Japanese commander had formally surrendered on the deck of the U.S.S. *Missouri,* in Tokyo harbor. Behind *Mako* were a half-dozen patrols since the Funabushi Harbor battle, patrols that had seen her, like all Allied submarines, prowling hundreds of miles of sea lanes to find targets.

The boat had cruised far up the channel and was approaching a sub tender gleaming with strings of lights. A signal flashed from the tender as *Mako* approached the nest of boats moored beside her. On the sub's bridge the quartermaster flashed a response with a signal light. The boat worked in slowly toward the submarine to which it would tie up. Standing by with the heevey-line, Keith threw it to one of the relief gang standing on the deck of the sub. He heard the captain's quiet command:

"All stop. Rudder amidships."

His throat tightened as he felt the final vibrations of the engines die under his feet. There was silence for a while. Then the forward hatch was thrown open, and down in the torpedo room he could hear men yelling as they started tricing everything up before going ashore.

One of the line-handlers on the other sub shouted at him. "Hey sailor! Is that *Mako?*"

"Affirmative on that!" Keith called back. "Heard of her?"

"You bet. Somebody said she was coming in. Pretty fair boat?"

"The best," Keith said.

The sailor inspected the scarred and scaling super-structure, and grinned. "Make her yourselves?" he asked.

"Yeah. From a kit!"

Keith gazed back at the damaged plates and

railings, and suddenly he was enormously proud of the old boat. She had taken them out, and she had brought them back. She had performed feats no submarine was expected to perform. They would not forget her at Guadalcanal nor at New Guinea. Nor would the men who had sailed from Mare Island on her ever forget her, for although they had not made her, she had truly made them—into the proud and independent sailing men called submariners.

SOME NAVAL WORDS AND PHRASES

abaft: behind or farther aft

aft: in, near, or toward the stern of a vessel

arm: to make ready to explode; torpedoes arm themselves by the turning of a propeller as they run toward the target.

ashcan: a depth charge

aye, aye: reply to an order to indicate that it is understood and will be carried out. Does not necessarily mean "yes."

bearing: direction of an object in degrees clockwise around a circle. "Relative bearings" refers to an object's direction in relation to the course of the ship. An object directly ahead would be at 000 degrees. At right angles to the starboard beam (the widest point of the ship), it would be at 090 degrees, and so on around the circle to 360 degrees.

bilge: to fail. Also the lower part of a vessel where the waste water and seepage collect.

bridge: platform from which a ship is steered, navigated, and conned.

broach: to break unexpectedly into view from below the surface. Also, to turn broadside to the waves.

bullnose: a chock, or hole for mooring lines, at the extreme front of the submarine.

chief: a chief petty officer on a boat. Also called "CPO."

cigarette deck: a small deck abaft the bridge, where smoking is permitted.

COB: Chief of the Boat. The highest-ranking enlisted man on a submarine.

compartment: a room on a ship.

conn: to direct the ship by orders to the helmsman.

conning tower: the small compartment atop the submarine's pressure hull. From here, the boat can be directed while running beneath the surface. Although a part of the pressure hull, the conning tower can be sealed off completely and abandoned in case of severe damage. The boat is then directed from the control room.

control room: the compartment beneath the conning tower, containing all the main instruments and controls on the submarine.

deck: the floor, whether indoors or outdoors.

depth gauge: an instrument which tells how far beneath the surface the boat lies. (See "fathometer.")

door: an opening in a vertical surface on a ship. (See "hatch.")

echo-range: to send out vibrations which bounce

256

back from any ship or object in the area, betraying its presence to the ship that is "echo-ranging." Also known as "pinging."

executive officer: on a submarine, the officer second in command. Also called the "exec" or "X.O."

fathom: a six-foot unit of length.

fathometer: an instrument which tells the depth of the water beneath the submarine's keel.

freeing ports: openings in a submarine's outer hull.

gyro: a gyroscopic steering device in a torpedo, similar to an automatic pilot. A gyroscope keeps the rudder turned always in the same direction.

hatch: an opening in a deck, or horizontal surface.

heevey line: slang for "heaving line," a lightweight line attached to a heavier line too bulky to throw.

hull: the framework of a vessel, exclusive of rigging and superstructure.

instruct: to regulate a torpedo so that it will run true to the target.

JOD: junior officer of the deck.

knot: one nautical mile per hour. Equivalent to $1\frac{1}{8}$ m.p.h. on land.

main induction: the large pipe through which the boat's air is drawn while the boat is running on the surface. The boat's windpipe, so to speak.

pressure hull: the watertight shell of a submarine which houses the crew and equipment. It does not include the ballast tanks which comprise much of the familiar cigar-shape of the boat.

screws: propellers.

secure: to release from a duty or watch. "Secure the maneuvering watch."

smoking lamp: a lamp for lighting pipes on old-time ships. The phrase "the smoking lamp is lit" now indicates that men are allowed to smoke.

sonar stack: the equipment which forms the sonarman's station.

superstructure: all equipment and fittings extending above the deck.

TBT: "target bearing transmitter." A mounted spyglass on the bridge, on which a button is pressed when a target is in the lens, which automatically transmits the bearing to the conning tower.

TDC: torpedo data computer. A complex device which calculates how the gyros must be set to direct the torpedo to the target, and automatically sets them as the information is fed into it.

tin can: a destroyer.

trim: to balance the ship by flooding or venting buoyancy tanks.

vent: to force water from a buoyancy tank with compressed air.

A submarine has five main speeds forward. Commands for these speeds are given by the captain as follows:

all ahead⅓—about five knots on the surface.

all ahead ⅔—calls for a certain number of revolutions per minute of the engines, increasing the speed correspondingly.

all ahead standard

all ahead flank—top speed

all ahead emergency—The captain thinks the engine room can do a little better. At least they'd better try!

AUTHOR'S NOTE

Although U.S.S. *Mako* will not be found listed in
Fahey's *The Ships and Aircraft of the United States
Fleet*, there is nothing fanciful about the record that
my fictitious submarine achieves in these pages. No
extravagance is necessary in dramatizing the story
of the men who fought the submarine battles of
World War II. Heroism and humor, tragedy and
suspense glow through the official battle reports.
The subs went out, fought to the last torpedo, and
came back—God willing.

One man who fought in and survived the submarine war is John E. Lee, of Rancho Santa Fe,
California. Jack Lee, a calm man who now manages
an investment firm, retired only recently with the
rank of rear admiral, his last command being that of
Commodore of Submarine Flotilla One, based at
San Diego.

During World War II, Admiral Lee was a submarine commander in the Pacific theater of war and
had his share of thrilling experiences, including being left on the bridge when the submarine *Grayling*

submerged. He gave me some help a while ago on another book that I was writing, and as I talked with him I resolved some day to write a story of submarine warfare in the Pacific. This is the book that resulted.

I am deeply indebted to Admiral Lee for technical assistance, and for arranging a trip in a submarine which supplied firsthand knowledge that I could not have obtained otherwise.

A number of other Naval officers were helpful to me in the course of my research. But it is Navy policy—based perhaps on a feeling that, since submarine commanders do not ask authors how to run submarines, authors should reciprocate by not asking them how to write stories—that such help should be made unofficially. Nevertheless, informal guidance was made available to help me through the labyrinths of target tracking, diving procedure, and similar matters.

To Captain Thomas, commander of the submarine *Remora;* to Lieutenant Commander Kaltenborn, his executive officer; and to all the other men who aided me, I extend my grateful thanks.

Of the books consulted during the course of this work, the most valuable was the excellent official United States Naval Institute volume, *United States Submarine Operations in World War II,* by Theodore Roscoe. The war, as seen through the eyes of a submarine commander, is dramatically presented in two books by Captain Edward L. Beach, U.S.N., *Submarine!* and *Run Silent, Run Deep;* and in the book *War Fish* by George Grider and Lydel Sims.

A warm and exciting account of the enlisted man's war is recounted by Forest Sterling, in his book, *Wake of the Wahoo.*

Other works of great help were the official *Battle Report* series by Walter Karig and others; *The Battle of Midway,* by Irving Werstein; and *The Coastwatchers,* by Commander Eric A. Feldt.

BIBLIOGRAPHY

Beach, Edward L., *Run Silent, Run Deep,* Holt, Rinehart and Winston, Inc., New York, 1955.

Beach, Edward L., *Submarine!* Holt, Rinehart and Winston, Inc., New York, 1952.

Fahey, James C., *The Ships and Aircraft of the United States Fleet,* Ships and Aircraft, 1265 Broadway, New York, 1944.

Feldt, Eric A., *The Coastwatchers,* Oxford University Press, New York, 1946.

Grider, George, and Sims, Lydel, *War Fish,* Little, Brown and Company, Boston, 1958.

Morison, Samuel Eliot, *History of United States Naval Operations in World War II,* Vol. VIII, Little, Brown and Company, Boston, 1953.

Roscoe, Theodore, *United States Submarine Operations in World War II,* U.S. Naval Institute, Annapolis, Md., 1949.

Sterling, Forest J., *Wake of the Wahoo,* Chilton Company, Philadelphia, 1960.

Werstein, Irving, *The Battle of Midway,* Thomas Y. Crowell Company, New York, 1961.

ABOUT THE AUTHOR

FRANK BONHAM tells us that *"War Beneath the Sea . . .* involved a process of education for the author. I took a trip on a submarine; I sought out old submariners; I asked many questions of a retired admiral friend; I read thirty or forty books and spent six hours on a sub-tender. Writing is a continuous process of re-education, and that is one reason I love it."

Mr. Bonham, a native Californian by birth, began writing as soon as he left U.C.L.A. Since then, he has written over five hundred short stories and twenty novels—for adults as well as for young people. Mr. Bonham now lives in La Jolla with his wife and three sons.